The Bridge Keeper's Log Book:

For Michael

Poet + Friend

short stories
by Tom Bryan

T B

Biscuit Publishing
Competition
2011

November 2011

Published © 2011 by
Biscuit Publishing Ltd
PO Box 123
Washington
Newcastle upon Tyne
NE37 2YW
United Kingdom

www.biscuitpublishing.com

ISBN 978 1 903914 47 2

Typeset by Free Spirit Writers, Bridlington

Printed by Jasprint Ltd, Washington, NE37 2SH,
United Kingdom

Table of Contents

Dedication

To my father Orville (1912-1953) and my mother Betty (1923-1972). Extra thanks to Marcia Miles, my English teacher, who first encouraged me to write.

Acknowledgements

The author and publisher wish to acknowledge with thanks previous publication and/or broadcast of some of the stories in the following:

BBC Radio Scotland, BBC Radio Three, BBC Radio Four, the World Service, Happenstance Chapbook, New Writing Scotland, New Writing Dundee, Bridport Anthology, The Eildon Tree, Cutting Teeth, Biscuit Anthology, Harper Collins Short Story Anthology, Dream Catcher, Macallan Shorts Anthology. Nearly half the stories in this collection are previously unpublished.

I wish to thank Creative Scotland for a grant towards a future collection of themed short stories, five of which are published for the first time in this collection.

Thanks to Michael, Anna and Lis and to many other family and friends who have helped over the years.

Special thanks to Brian and all those at Biscuit Publishing for the practical encouragement given to poets and fiction writers over several years and to Ian Stephen in particular for his unselfish help and advice. A big thanks also to Janice Galloway for permission to use the quote on the back cover of the book.

Lyrics cited:
"Mama Said," The Shirelles, 1960.
"Long Line Rider," copyright Bobby Darin. 1968.
"Livin' Like a Trucker," copyright Rory Gallagher. 1973.
"A Million Miles Away," copyright Rory Gallagher. 1973.

Angry Blood

A black man walks through the slums of Madrid, wearing a false beard and Groucho Marx moustache. If I had been there, I would have seen through his disguise, the way children do. *I know you. You're Floyd Patterson; I've seen you on television.*

When I was ten, our new television was a novelty on the street. We watched the poor reception from under a tent made from a blanket draped over two chairs. I saw a big white man knock Patterson to the canvas.

"Patterson's a coward, no wonder he's hiding somewhere," said my older brother. "As a kid in New York he used to hide in the dark, sleep in cinemas, subways and old sheds."

"Hiding doesn't mean you're a coward. It could mean he's just shy."

"Then shy men shouldn't be boxers."

Tell me about it. I was watching TV from under a blanket. Peace, just like sleeping in a summer tent with a soft rain falling, breeze billowing the sides. Cupboards the same, letting the clothes drape over you.

If Floyd Patterson was a coward then I was too.

On the street is noise like radio static. Ukrainian noise has lots of "sh" and "zh" in it; Quebecois is frantic, like a small bird in a cage and some of it is directed at me. I can run and hide too. I hide in the slough in a cottonwood hut, curved branches; the only noise the grey jays and the geese overhead, redwing blackbirds trying to clear the syrup from their throats. Dogs barking, sleepy, far away.

I persisted with my boxing hero who was real, maybe too real with his blood and swollen eyes. Our heroes then were unreal. Jungle Jim. Rin-Tin-Tin, Lassie, Superman.

I tried to explain.

"He was hurt. There is nothing wrong with being hurt. You ever been hurt?"

"Aw, go run and hide, just like a coward."

I had to get on with my life before I saw Patterson again. Same white man. The champion, Ingemar Johansson. That night, Patterson had a different look. He waded in and the big Swede went straight down. I cheered wildly.

"You'll be happy now. Patterson won. He won't have to hide, until after the next time."

Johansson lay on the canvas, bloodied, still. Patterson breaks free from his cheering corner, kisses the white man's forehead, and cradles his head like a child's. Ringside medics come to his aid. Patterson's face has the concern of a parent for a hurt child. Nobody else had seen it. His boxing trainers had despaired of him ever becoming a killer, a punching machine. "We just can't anger his blood," they said. Angry blood. Patterson didn't have it.

The black boy is hungry, far too young to be on his own. He rides the subway. He should be in school. His thick wool jacket is pulled as tight as it can go. The wool hat is pulled down over the ears, as low to the eyes as possible. Knees tucked up. The boy sits in the cinema through several showings. He laughs at Slip Mahoney and the Bowery Boys. He loves Curly, Larry and Moe. He is hungry but does not go home yet. At a subway station he climbs a rickety ladder and climbs into a workman's empty tool shed. He thinks he is a coward. He loves sitting in the shed when it is raining outside. He does not fear the rat feet overhead. He is not afraid of the dark or anything in the dark. The tiny rat feet sound like rain.

I am now 12, Patterson is only 27, an old 27.

"Watch this carefully punk. See what happens to your hero tonight."

Sonny Liston is scary. He rips Patterson apart. Corners him, closes in for the kill. Patterson looks utterly alone.

Before the tears came, I fled to the cupboard, my head covered by my mother's Hudson's Bay fur coat. It was warm and familiar. Nobody would look for me there.

Meanwhile, a lonely black man walks through the Madrid slums at night. False beard, false moustache. He wants to find a dark place, safe and warm, where nobody in the world can find him.

A Cat Named Lonesome

Here's how I began "disappearances": the rubber letters slide into a tray. The tray is on a small metal roller. There is a crank at the side. I turn the crank. The rubber letters pass through some ink and the words come out on a sheet of paper. Sometimes the letters are upside down, front to back or smudged. I am just a kid. What do you expect? Here are the disappearances I have so far, all produced on my Hudson's Bay Kiddo Printing Press *(Kids, print your very own newspaper!)*

PUFFY

My black and brown puppy. I couldn't say "puppy" properly. He left. I talked for three days about him coming back. After three days there is no more talk about Puffy. Three days is all you are allowed to talk about puppies that are gone. *Dead* says my brother. After three days means *dead*. And you shouldn't talk about the dead.

Sports Section
MICHAEL KOROLENKO

Our world's greatest ice hockey goaltender. He grew up just down the street. *World famous* – in Canada. "Beyond the pale," hissed my grandfather. "What does that mean? Is it like disappearing?" "In a way," replied grandfather, popping a strong imperial mint into his mouth, because my grandmother now barred him chewing tobacco. I think he meant Michael had some recent problems which prevented him from being the world's greatest ice hockey goalie. "Either his problems will vanish or he will," said my uncle. In a way, it's a race between a man and his problems to see who will win.

THE LIST IS GROWING

It sure is.

Grandfather, who farmed 1600 acres of wheat for over fifty years but never went to school much. He gave me $10 for some paper and ink. He liked my newspaper and read every issue. Except this one, because he has since disappeared the way that dead people do.

Grandmother too, who once met Sitting Bull in person, but that is a story for another time. Sitting Bull has vanished.

My other uncle also, who was exploded in World War Two.
A real bad disappearance.

My father, into a pine coffin.

My mother into a pine coffin, next to his pine coffin.

The pine wood was not from an old tree. Father and mother
were both younger than the tree. Tree and people will disappear
together but at different rates.

All this done on a child's printing press a long time ago. The
ink ran out. The rubber shredded. The small metal handle broke
off. The whole mess got thrown out in a shoe box. It is gone.

Twenty Years Later

Now, the main story, written on an Adler typewriter that is
nearly too heavy for a young man to lift. It is over two decades
later but disappearance is still the theme. Very much so.

"A Cat Named Lonesome"

Red socks, white sink.

White sink, red socks. Steeping, soaking.

Drain the sink, wring the socks, grey water down the drain.

Fill the sink for a rinse. Cold water. Red socks bright in the
clear water.

The poet left a hungry cat named "Lonesome" who is purring
around the ankles of any person about to feed him. The cat's
nose is in the feed dish before the cat food is forked into the dish
so that Lonesome has cat food on his whiskers. He doesn't care,
clearly doesn't mind. The bowl is divided in two, for food and
water. Lonesome doesn't go to the water so he must not be
thirsty. Ah, the sink where the socks are. He could have got up
there for a drink?

*   *   *

From the Golden Gate Bridge, the water is sparkling in the July
sun. It ripples in the breeze. The man seeing this is a poet and
painter so he won't miss much from up there. Matthew Arnold
once said the Celts as a people "rebel against the tyranny of
fact," and I wonder if the poet looking at the dancing water is
rebelling against these facts:

*There are 206 bones in the human body and any or all or most of
them may be broken in the jump.*

*Depending on factors such as height and weight, the jumper will be
travelling between 76 and 90 miles per hour before impact.*

The bridge is roughly 260 feet above the water.

The jump will last about four seconds.

A common cause of death is the jumper's internal bleeding or ruptured spleen.

For a poet, it is not an original final choice; the Golden Gate Bridge is the number one location in the world for suicides.

It will be thirty years after the poet's decision until anybody survives the attempt intact and is able to swim to shore.

Drowning and hypothermia are common.

There have been about 1200 suicides since the bridge opened. However, this is a conservative estimate.

Many bodies are never found, due to currents and undertows, fog and darkness.

The odds of surviving the jump are less than two per cent, which is not the same as surviving for very long afterwards. You may survive the jump but will probably die in the ambulance or hospital.

If the poet squints into the sun, he will see Baker's Beach, where in four more years a young swimmer aged 18 will be killed by a great white shark, despite the young man's girlfriend's heroic efforts to save him. A shark usually needs to be about 15 feet long before its jaws are strong enough to attack a human without harm to the jaws. Sharks somehow know this.

More facts: they tag (electronically) huge sharks and find that some of them do regularly swim under the Golden Gate Bridge.

If your body breaks and bleeds (as is likely) then it is also likely that the big sharks will be aware of your blood.

Meanwhile, police found the 1954 Plymouth Savoy with the keys in the ignition but passport and savings book gone. That's about all we know.

We also all know we too will vanish. We must prepare for it. Sometimes we don't have enough time to do this right. Hence, red socks steeping in a white sink and a hungry cat named Lonesome, who fed or not will still fade away. Our planet is not a cat but we could still call it Lonesome.

Heartless, in Saint Boniface

(Sheet 2: The Hudson's Bay 'Kiddo' Printing Press, January 1957. The press "office" was the kitchen table. The paper's circulation never topped six).

SPECIAL ISSUE: MISSING BODY PARTS
A human leg came flying down the stairs! I was playing with Lenny and Michael Pavelchuk. I heard a roar from upstairs. It was their father Pavel. He swore. In Ukrainian I think, then threw his leg down the stairs. I told my mother. She laughed. She told me it was just a plaster cast. Pavel cut the plaster off with a knife and threw it down the stairs. I've heard that sometimes people find arms and legs and heads and stuff. After bears get them, or sharks. As editor of this newspaper, my opinion? I think human beings are just like that. We go missing and so do parts of us.

Here's what's useful. Corneas. Hearts. Livers. Kidneys. Lungs. Blood. Tissue.

Item of interest: Bend your arm at the elbow, holding it upright. That's how big the Russian monk Rasputin's dick was! It's in a jar in a Russian museum. I saw a dick that big once but it belonged to a donkey.

My pocket money goes missing just like body parts. Larry Charbonneau hides in the bushes with his brother Gabe. Larry jumps out, kicks me in the shins. Gabe takes my money. They run for the Provencher Bridge and vanish into the crooked streets of Saint Boniface. They like their Patisserie. My money has vanished. The tasty French pastries have also vanished. Larry and Gabe are getting rather chubby, at my expense. Unfortunately, Larry and Gabe Charbonneau haven't vanished. I see them right now, waiting for me.

Much later, I got a job with the little-known branch of the United Nations Department of Disappearances, Historical Unit, Division of Body Parts. You heard me right. I was given an assignment by our boss Erland Torvik, whom we called a man of few words.

"Carney. Tell me what you know about what we do. In as few words as possible."

12

"Sir, in many parts of the world, people are being murdered for the profitable trade in body parts. Some regimes even make pretence of capital punishment in order to harvest various parts and organs. This unit exists to halt this practice."

"Excellent Carney. How despicable can human beings get? But we can't turn you loose on the recently dead until you hone your skills on the less recently dead. Give me some insights on these. "

He threw a folder on my desk.

"Carney, you've got a week to add to the bibliographic wheel."

The folder said:

CROMWELL'S HEAD

At first, I puzzled over the scholarship, names, dates, allegations, gaps in the historical record. I had nearly used up all my time and had done nothing. Then, I returned to my earliest years as an editor and journalist, with my child's printing press. The cold lino. The smell of boiling cabbage and ham. The ice sheathed on the windows.

Then it became easier. Stick to the facts. Keep it clear, nearly child-like. How would the Kiddo Press would have reported it? In the same vein as the Pavel Pavelchuk incident.

Oliver Cromwell was famous. He was pretty ugly too, with warts. He was buried a hero but was dug up later. His enemies cut off his head and stuck in on a pole. A storm blew it off the pole. A captain found the head and hid it. He left it to his daughter when he died. It showed up in shows all over England. An actor owned it and tried to sell it but nobody wanted it, not even Cromwell's old college. A few more people bought the head. A family bought the head and kept it until 1960 when they gave it to Cromwell's college who this time took it. They gave it a secret and proper burial somewhere in the college grounds. The head was rolling around in history from 1685 to 1960. When it became a skull instead of a head we do not know.

I gave the Kiddo report to Few Words Torvik and he said:

"I like your sparse style. Try another."

Over to the Kiddo Press:

MATA HARI

Mata Hari's real name was Margaretha Zelle. She was beautiful. She was a dancer. She was also a spy. She was born in Holland. She was executed by the French in 1917. Usually, they cut off the heads of anyone shot by a firing squad. Her head was put in a Paris museum. When the museum moved somewhere else, the head went missing. It is still missing. Someone somewhere in Paris may have a skull. Can skulls be as beautiful as the women they come from?

"Not bad Carney. She turned heads then lost hers. For good. Try this."

THOMAS PAINE (1737-1809)

A la Kiddo:

Tom Paine hated Kings and Queens. He liked ordinary people. He helped the Americans get enough courage to fight the King of Britain, and win. Paine was not welcome in England where he came from. The French liked him because he hated the King of Britain. But the French put him in jail. He went back to America. They now didn't like him much either because they said he didn't believe in God. In America, you must believe in God or at least pretend to. He was buried in America. Then he was taken back to England for re-burial. Somewhere between New York and Norfolk his remains went missing. His bones are still missing. He is now once more a hero in America. Even the English think he was a great man. His father was a Quaker and made corsets for women, out of whale bone. Bones played a big part in the Paine family.

"Not bad Carney, not bad at all. One more to go."

JOHN PAUL (JONES)

His father was a Scottish gardener. John ran off to sea and later worked on a slave ship. When the Americans fought the British, he won many battles. To one nation he was a hero, to the other, a traitor and a pirate. He started the American Navy. Later, he started the Russian Navy and was also their hero. He went to France and died. He was buried in a cemetery for Protestants which later became a dumping ground for dead dogs. Much later, it became a gambling site. They found his grave in 1905 and took his remains back to America for a hero's burial. From 1792 until 1905 his remains were lost.

"Carney, well done. Anybody who writes this way won't get all sentimental and self-indulgent. It would only get in the way of the important work we are doing. I think we can proceed now with more relevant field work. I think you're ready."

"Indirectly, I owe everything I learned to Pavel Pavelchuk."

"Should I be familiar with his work, Carney?"

"You won't be sir. Pavelchuk was more a man of action."

"But Carney, what did he know of missing body parts?"

"Plenty. He fought in World War Two."

Invisible on Saint John's Avenue

Kiddo Printing Press, continued, circa 1957. Special "Invisibility" issue

On our street, it would sometimes be good to be invisible. Here comes Digger Doig. Digger is a huge lumpy boy who does mud. He cultivates his own backyard mud and frog marches you to it. He grabs your neck.

"Eat mud punk. Tell me how good it tastes. Go on punk . . ."

"Tastes great Digger. Nothing better. Yum, yum . . ." and so on.

The two brothers, Ivan and Pavel, are like wasps in the hedges. They buzz out. They sting you with kicks and punches but are more like honey bees than wasps, as they extract your pocket money like pollen from your pockets.

Step right up ladies and gentlemen; here on Saint John's Avenue, invisibility for sale, only kind and decent people need apply.

I have an upended wooden box which once contained apples. It is my street stall. I have many items of invisibility for sale.

Caps, helmets, cloaks, shirts, rings, pills, potions.

"Hey, this cap looks good."

"Yeah, it's modelled on Alberich's Tarnkappe. He was a little German whose cap made its wearer invisible. Trouble is, the cap itself stays visible so a well-aimed kick or punch just below the cap would do the business." I shuddered to think of Doig getting hold of the cap. An invisible Doig. A bit like a shark with an extra set of jaws.

"Best not to have a visible cloak, cap or helmet that doesn't itself become invisible. How about pills and potions?"

"Fern seed, heliotrope. Even sassafras. Same thing. As they wear off, you become visible and get hammered for what you did when invisible. Imagine aiming a kick at Doig only to become fully visible to him mid-kick! Also, it's hard to know how long these potions last and when they take effect. They might have nasty side effects."

"Some say a chameleon stuffed down your shirt could make you invisible."

"Timmy Douglas has a chameleon and he's one of the most visible guys I know."

Timmy's mother had recently put him on a diet.

"There's magic stones you can carry in your pocket."

"Wouldn't work. Washing machines. Holes in the pocket. I would forget it was there. Would my trousers become invisible? Would the washing machine? Would my mother who empties my trouser pockets before putting stuff in the washer?"

"Rings are a good bet. A long time ago there was the Ring of Gyges. It had to be turned inward to work. The shepherd who found it became rich and powerful."

"Turn inward? What does that mean? How do you turn a ring inside out? It must have been made of paper or something. Anything simpler?"

"Put any ring on a finger. Then make a fist so that the invisible part of you covers up the visible part. Anyway, Reynard's Ring was ideal. It had three gemstones or one gem with three colours. Red turned night into day. White cured any disease or illness. Green made you invisible."

"Sounds messy. How do you control which colour? Suppose being invisible is a disease? One part of the ring would destroy the other part."

"I don't know really. I guess invisibility has a lot of problems with it."

During my day on the stall, I realised that not all of my customers would put the gift to a noble use. Linda Ravinelli's bedroom was mentioned a lot, though not as much as ice hockey. Imagine being invisible coming down the wing against Montreal Canadienne? I suppose they would just play the puck and forget the winger. Shop-lifting came high on the list. Staying out late too. But some bullies would become even better ones by being invisible. I decided to give up on the idea. We didn't need any invisibility on Saint John's Avenue. Best to keep all the nasty stuff out in the open.

However, I remember my grandmother once told me about the Lakota Ghost Shirt. She was a little white girl on the Dakota prairie when a Paiute prophet named Wovoka said he learned in a vision of a special song and dance which would make the white people disappear and the buffalo return. The ghost shirt was later added for extra protection, like a bullet proof vest. In some cases it would make the singer and dancer invisible to the white men and their bullets. She remembered seeing the old Lakota men after the Ghost Dance had died out. Unfortunately, the shirt hadn't worked at Wounded Knee. She was sad about this as a little girl. She was even sadder about it near the end of her life.

16

But perhaps it did work? Although the buffalo never returned, neither did my grandmother and all her white family. They all later died — then became invisible. This is what the Ghost Shirt dancers wanted, before they too vanished forever to hunt their invisible buffalo somewhere. Take your pick then. Rings, helmets, cloaks, potions. Given time, they all finally work.

Snow Bird

I can't peel an orange without a smile for my late Uncle Travis Mackay. "Mackay" is a good Caithness name right enough, but his forebears left Caithness three generations earlier for the equally treeless Canadian prairies. "Travis" is a hardy name, just right for 60 years of fire, lightning, horseflies and all the grief farming 1600 acres of hard wheat can dish out. He farmed until he could farm no more but I can tell you how we — Uncle Travis and me — once fought for our true North and won. I'll tell you this in the time it takes to peel an orange and probably throw most of it away. I never liked oranges much anyway. Neither did Travis.

I was managing a citrus and olive farm in southern Spain at the time. What can I say? The sky was the silly blue that children do with big wax crayons. Lemons just fell into the dust and rotted. I could never get used to the sun, the blue sky and those fat lemons looking like some wayward child had made them up. But then, I grew up in Cold Moose, Saskatchewan, population 273, including Travis, *especially* including Travis.

I was sitting in the shade of a lime tree, drinking a cold "San Miguel," wondering if I should retire for good down here in Andalusia, among the bougainvillea and orange blossom, when the letter thumped like a migraine onto my zebrawood table.

Dear Donald,

Travis has been expelled, yes *expelled,* from the Sons of the Pioneers Home for the Elderly for, among other things:

chewing tobacco at night in bed!

keeping a loaded shotgun in his wardrobe!

digging up the Home's floral borders and re-planting with cabbages and spinach!

Far from being upset or contrite, Travis is now living in a shack he has built outside our old house in Cold Moose, on the fringes of the rugby pitch, in full sight of the workers' hostel. I fear the Rural Municipalities Office won't tolerate his presence there much longer. He is a squatter. Donald, cousin, I don't really need this at my age. Can't you get him to retire to one of those lovely Florida rest homes to see out his final years in sunshine and peace? I know — as all of us do — that you always were your Uncle Travis' favourite nephew...

God, the Clash of the Titans. Nadine (it rhymes with "warrior queen") was a younger version of her father, stubborn, implacable, the raiser of one eyebrow at a time and when that eyebrow went up, any opponent was vanquished. I sighed and looked at the cruel blue Andalusian sky. I would be caught between the two of them. I would be torn to shreds by my own kinfolk.

Sure, I was Travis' favourite for many reasons. He dearly loved my father, his youngest of six brothers, and wept constantly for nearly two years after my father was killed in a car crash when I was seven. Travis also knew I could be trusted (for shiny Canadian dimes) to fetch his favourite chewing tobacco at the corner shop, when it had been denied him for health reasons. Both wheat farmers and coal miners adopted chewing tobacco to replace cigarettes, which were forbidden at work as a fire hazard. But back to Nadine's letter:

"Since you work for Citrus Systems International" with citrus concerns in California, Florida and Spain and your company also owns several properties in Florida, get Uncle Travis a house down in Florida, and meanwhile, get a flight over here and get Travis out of his shack into a plane and into one of your retirement homes. We'll pay for it. Price is no object but family pride is. A squatter! A squatter! My own father.

Your loving cousin, Nadine

Help me! My company does own Sewanee Retirement Villas in Sunnydale, Florida. A parcel of pastel prefabs, fronted by indentikit palm trees, bloated security systems, access to supermarkets, beach frontage, mini-golf, fishing, etc. The idea of getting Travis into one of these places rocks me with laughter. As much chance as this fat orange dripping its sticky juice between my fingers turning into a big hard snowball. Travis could swear like no man who ever lived but there were only two words that he ever said with such a sneer your guts churned over when he said it. *Snow Bird. I'll never in my life be one of them effin Snow Birds:* Canadians and Northern Americans who quit fighting snow and hail and retire to Florida, Arizona and California to die in the sun. *To sit around and rot in the sun* said Travis. *Effin Snow Birds.* A reasonable enough human thing to do, to just sit in the sun like I was doing the day Nadine's letter came. However, I did as I was told and took the first flight over. I made my way to my Uncle's shack sandwiched between the house where he used to live, the rugby field and the high-rise hostels for imported oil workers. The Canadian Pacific tracks shimmered beyond. The shack was about the size of a tool shed and it was fronted by another shed, his outhouse. There were already people gathered.

"He won't talk to us."

"Says he has a loaded shotgun."

"Says we had better leave him in peace."

I knock loudly and stand back.

No answer.

I knock again. "Travis. Uncle Travis. Open up. It's your favourite nephew, Donald Mackay."

I knock louder. I wait. There is a grey rain falling, winter is not so far away on the prairie, the clouds are rolling, fast and dark, like a river in spate.

I turn to go.

I hear the door creak open at my back. The crowd gasps.

"Quick, son! Come in! Quick!"

Travis bolted the door. "Got any chaw with you?" I handed him a few tobacco tins. I look around quickly. A table and two chairs. One window. A camping gas cooker, two rings. A gas heater. Candle flickering on the table. Travis is a tall bony man. If he stuck his tongue out, he'd look like a zipper. He motions to a chair.

"Hi, lard ass. Did Nadine send you here?"

I've only been in his shack two minutes and I've already been given the dreaded raised eyebrow! I notice how dark Travis is. Travis always proudly claimed Cree blood. When I was a boy, he spoke to me in Cree and I assumed every adult did that. He was doing it right now.

A we na ka pa sit e sa hoosk?

(Something like, who sent you?

My Cree is rusty but I try. **Mona ni ke skein ne tain** (*I don't know*).

That bleeping Nadine, eh?

"You know I can't walk out of here without you coming with me, Travis."

"You'll have to."

"Travis, you *can't* stay here. That mob is ready to tear the place down and have you arrested as a squatter. The next rugby match will clear you off anyway."

He spit a big gob of tobacco juice into an empty coffee can.

20

"Where you taking me, nephew, back to that Old Pioneers Death Bed?"

"No Travis, down to Florida..."

"Travis Mackay? An effin Snow Bird? "

And the hair stood up on my neck the way he said those two words, like something vile. I knew then the whole thing was one big ridiculous lie. Travis would never leave this shack, alive anyway.

Travis, who had once piled his furniture onto the Canadian Pacific tracks in order to halt the train and steal its coal to keep his family alive that winter.

Travis, who had been hit by lightning four times in 60 years and whose left eyelid still juddered sometimes as a result.

Travis, who had farmed sixty years in flood, fire, influenza, lightning, and snow blizzards, making a profit only five of those sixty years.

Our Canadian national anthem said *Our True North Strong and Free* and here it was staring me in the face, eyebrows raised fiercely and its spit plinking into a coffee tin.

And I had been summoned here from Spain to get this man to retire to Florida!

I watched his shadow flicker in the candlelight, his long fingers cupped around his head like a man sheltering from the sun. Outside, the wind howled. The people had gone home. I stayed the night on the floor. The last words I heard him say before sleep were in Cree: *Ne ke ke wan* — *I want to go home.*

I peeked out through the filthy curtains in the morning. It was snowing lightly. God help us! Nadine was circling the shack like a vulture. She shouted at the window.

"You two had better walk out together, straight to the airport, with two one-way tickets to Orlando Beach."

I threw the door open, practically taking Nadine's arm away with the force of it. "You're by yourself" she screamed. Where the hell is that bleep bleepin bleep of a bleep. . ."

Then, the old "bleep" came out meekly just behind me, his hair combed neatly. He carried a small suitcase. We walked a gauntlet between shocked friends, relatives and public officials.

The end of the story? Remember, *this* is *Travis Mackay* we're talking about.

We got to Florida all right. I set Travis up in a company bungalow, got him golfing and fishing, bought him a snazzy pair of Bermuda shorts and a blue Hawaiian shirt with bright yellow pineapples on it. Nadine only came down once to Florida to check on Travis but we knew she wouldn't come again. She had won. Getting rid of Travis had kept the family dignity and pride intact and she would now have better things to do. Fortunately, she really detested phones and this was long before the days of email. Travis could live out his life in peace and he did, eventually.

Years before, that night in his small squatter's shack up in Cold Moose, Travis and I had hit upon a plan, *True North* we called it, and the plan worked perfectly right up to the time Travis died three years ago. We had stuck an old man, John Brown, rent-free in the Florida bungalow and supplied him with a lifetime supply of aerogrammes, written and signed by Travis himself, dated for several years in the future. John was instructed to post one off every week or so:

Dear Nadine,

Loving the sun, the golf, the fishing. I'm so glad you got me to see the error or my ways. No snow, no hail, no forty below zero. I guess I've become a Snow Bird after all, and it's not so bad. "

Yours truly, Travis

Meanwhile, Travis himself was about two thousand miles to the north, living in an old logger's cabin outside Whitefish, Saskatchewan, a good several hundred miles north of his own beloved Cold Moose. When he died, we had him buried in his preferred permafrost. Nadine was happy enough to have him buried up in Canada. He could no longer embarrass her though she must have wondered at the speed a body could be transported from Florida to Saskatchewan! She never discovered our ploy. She still crows how she got Travis "to see sense and enjoy the last years of his life in the sunshine." Some northern friends of my uncle's kept the deception up right to the end, even telling Nadine the details of how they had "arranged" for the body to be flown north. They'd even managed to dodge officialdom, coroners, etc. However, I'd forgotten one important thing— the thin blue aerogrammes!

Dear Nadine,

The weather has really been great and I have never been so happy and comfortable as I am right now. This Florida bungalow is as snug as a coffin. I could wish nothing more than to stay just as I am, forever.

Love,
Travis "Snow Bird" Mackay

The letter was postmarked nearly a month after we had buried Travis in the same earth where he had planted wheat for sixty years! Nadine couldn't deny that the signature was authentic. I guess she just assumed the letter had got held up in the post and that her forgetful father had got the date wrong. I told old John Brown he should now burn the rest of the aerogrammes. He told me he cremated them on a cold Florida day. Just as he put a match to them, he looked up to see a big flock of wild geese returning home — returning north.

Shell Shock

The room was full of dinosaurs and tigers, rows of shoes, a thick Hudson's Bay fur parka and a pair of bright red earmuffs. Who lived under the earmuffs? Theodore, thin, not tall, grinning, age-less, hair like a pair of curtains parted, bryl-creamed upwards. Thick glasses like prisms hiding the dark darting eyes behind them. In the winter (and it always seemed winter) he wobbled side-to-side, penguin-like, to the corner shop for pipe tobacco, his daily newspaper and paint supplies. He was my friend's uncle and we were allowed in his room occasionally. Theodore grinned and talked. Children were his best audience.

"How do you know so many dinosaurs, Theodore?"

"I don't just know their names. I paint what I saw, what I see. All I know or ever can be is what I taste and what I see," he said, as he finished the red slash of a Tyrannosaurus mouth.

"There were a lot of these in the war. The stegosaurs and triceratops were useful too, adding a bit of armoured defensive cover." He brushed them into the war scene as well.

The children giggled and guffawed.

"Aw Theodore, you never really saw that stuff in the war. There wasn't dinosaurs in the war."

"Kids, now, I saw plenty of them. Huge teeth, great claws. I paint what I see."

"Tigers too?"

"Especially tigers. They lived deep in the jungles of Burma and we had guard dogs trained to sniff out enemy snipers behind the lines. A sniper is someone who wants to shoot you from a tree. When the dogs barked, I went out to the edge of the jungle to see what was going on. And there he was, eyes like burning matches. Then, the tiger ran away. My dog barked only at tigers, snipers and cobras."

"Who would win, Theodore, in a fight between a tiger and a tyrannosaurus?"

Theodore paused his brush in mid-air.

"Can't say. Never saw them fight. I only paint what I saw or see, but I never saw them fight so I can't paint that. I didn't *see* it."

Theodore had come to his sister's house just before the end of the war, for *rest and recuperation* he said. He asked to stay for only a few days, but he was still there a few months later when her own husband returned from the war. Because they would need the space for their future children, Theodore would have to leave, maybe go into a hospital or rest home for treatment. But the years came and went and Theodore stayed on in the spare room, with his shoes, his parka, his red earmuffs and his collection of dinosaurs and tigers.

His brother-in-law finally got used to the idea.

"Aw hell, Ted never done any harm, no harm at all and he keeps himself to himself. Harmless. *Sad* maybe, but harmless."

Everybody around Theodore turned grey and old, paunchy and balding but he stayed young and continued painting tigers and dinosaurs. The children grew up and had children of their own who came to visit Theodore in turn. He told them the same thing. That he only painted what he really saw. In the war. A long time ago.

This all went on and is probably still going on, except for one rare hour in one rare day when I was about ten. Hoovers were hard to come by in that post-war street where nearly every house had several children tracking in mud, leaves and snow. Theodore's sister's vacuum cleaner was a beauty, an *Electrolux Upright*, bright orange and silver, its many attachments shiny and impressive.

It was a glorious autumn day; the maples and birches rattling a crisp beat in the wind. Theodore was already on the street, grinning, with a newspaper under his arm. "A great day for *it*," one of those things Theodore always said. I was sent home early from school with the chicken pox. I was at home and just sitting down to a cup of sugared tea and a peanut butter cookie when the phone rang. My mother answered.

"Hmm, yes. I'll get there right away".

She turned to me with some panic in her eyes.

"Grab your coat. Can't leave you in the house alone. This should be . . . uh, interesting."

We belted out the door. She pulled my arm taut. Down the street we flew to the house where Theodore stayed. The children were all away and his sister and her husband were both working, leaving Theodore alone as they had done for many years.

"Out back!" gasped Mrs. Rebrov. "Out back!" She was the one who had phoned my mother.

I had a clear view what was going on, since my mother had to leave me as she ran over to Theodore. He was in his old army coat, which had rarely been removed from the peg on his bedroom door. He wore his flat cloth cap and his red earmuffs. In the sparse prairie garden were propped up all his canvases, in a circle. Dinosaurs with gaping red mouths, ponderous brontosaurs, slavering tigers. Theodore running around the garden, shouting in a shrill high voice which wasn't his normal speaking voice. He was shouting orders to someone or something.

"Take cover, take cover. I won't let them get you!"

He had his sister's new Hoover under his arm like a bazooka. It was connected to a socket in the kitchen with a long electrical extension. He was attacking the falling leaves, scooping them up just before they hit the ground. Grin gone, grimacing, drenched in sweat, ashen-faced.

Someone unplugged the hoover. My mother led a shivering Theodore back towards the house. The tigers and dinosaurs followed him with their eyes. A bitter winter was coming.

Leshy Darko

I should not have tied a pretty blonde Ukrainian girl named Sasha to a tree and left her there to cry, for it was then my troubles really began.

On our post-war Canadian street, mothers warned their children in all the tongues of the Diaspora to stay away from the Canadian Pacific tracks and never ever to cross them, on pain of punishments we could not even begin to imagine. We were told this story in every language from Inverness to Spitzbergen, Kiev to Haifa. Me? I was told in pure Glaswegian: "If youse ever go across they bluidy tracks Ah'll skelp yer arse sae hard ye'll no sit doon fer a bluidy week, so Ah wull." My pal Hughie McFadyen's mother had another version of this. "Ah'll skelp yer gob sae hard ye'll hae tae eat through yer neb." Hughie reckoned he would rather eat through his mouth than through his nose, so he was an obedient boy.

Down the west end of our street, the Canadian Pacific tracks had became our frontier, our Berlin Wall, terra incognito, a lacuna on the knowledge of our city, Winnipeg, which we already knew was Cree Indian for "Muddy Water." A forbidden area, hence we yearned to know it, to taste its dangers. But we understood our parents' fears. We often flattened coins on the train tracks; shiny nickels and dimes became silver pancakes; we imagined what a boy would look like after a hundred box cars of the Canadian Pacific had passed over him. But it wasn't just the tracks. There was a canal and skating slough (slew) to drown in and a mysterious park called Korolenko Park where allegedly, bad things could happen to boys and girls. We weren't sure what those bad things were but wanted to find out.

Most of the houses west of the tracks were older, more run down, "war houses" built hastily during the war, ramshackle two storeys. Our newer houses were tidy pastel bungalows built to accommodate the inner city overspill, plus the swollen refugee immigrant population and were named "peace-time houses." There you have it. War and Peace, and our parents had all had enough of war, whichever side they'd fought on.

East down our street was the new brick Elementary School with the lovely Canadian flag fluttering (the pre-Maple Leaf one). There was a playground there. The grounds were safe and tidy. There were no trains and not much traffic, so parents could generally keep an eye on us. "East" in that post-war housing estate represented the East all our parents had known: they had all come from the East somewhere in Europe. The Ukraine, Poland, Russian, Germany, Scotland, Ireland. They knew "East." To them West meant uncertainty, risk, danger, harm. The endless prairie. Fierce native peoples. Barren wilderness. Our city was founded by fur trappers who in their own lingo said "Gone West" meaning "dead." So, on bicycles and tricycles, we stayed East and our parents were happy.

Hughie and I were good boys until we tied a wee Ukrainian girl named Sasha Churchenko to one of the few trees in our neighbourhood and accidentally forgot about her. The upshot is, her mother came looking for her and found her sobbing at the tree. She came hunting for me and Hughie. Our mothers did all the front door negotiations in that neighbourhood but the dads did the punishment and Hughie and I were both leathered for it. We took it in our heads to find Sasha and apologise profusely. We even had some chocolate as a peace offering. The chocolate was the nice kind my auntie Jean had brought from Edinburgh. There was no chocolate in our city quite like it. It was a big sacrifice. All we knew was that Sasha Churchenko lived somewhere near Korolenko Park, *across the tracks.*

Hughie and I knew we were both born into the wrong century. We hadn't tied Sasha up for any other reason than that we had captured her fairly and had taken her prisoner. We were Indians and she was our blonde captive. After all, our city was founded by native peoples, fur trappers, traders and long-distance voyageurs. We played out their history every day. We even wrote about them:

Jed Campbell and Broken Hand McClintock were gathering saskatoon berries one day in the Rocky Mountain foothills. Grizzly bears like saskatoons too. A huge female grizzly was gathering the berries with her two cubs. Broken Hand decided to go back to their camp and left Jed alone gathering berries . . .

We went to the edge of the tracks and stood by the level crossing, watching a hundred boxcars fly past, tailed by a bright red caboose. We drew our breaths, Hughie crossed himself, and we walked across the tracks into forbidden territory. We saw the houses, their paint peeling like blistered skin. Untethered dogs roamed around the tracks. "Everything smells like cabbage," said Hughie, who did have a good sense of smell. We both saw the forbidden canal and slough ringed by stringy willows. Then we walked home, feeling braver. We planned our next foray carefully. We took sandwiches, tins of cream soda and packets of whole sunflower seeds which were the neighbourhood treat. The neighbourhood boys pretended the big foiled pouches were really full of chewing tobacco. We took the two special chocolate bars as peace offerings to Sasha. We put these in Hughie's Scout pack. It was a quiet Saturday, few children were out playing yet. We went to the tracks; the level crossing barriers were open. We crossed the tracks. The canal was peaceful, ringed with bulrushes. Redwing blackbirds sang from the willows. The slough would be perfect for ice skating and we vowed to come back in winter to play hockey.

Then we walked down into Korolenko Park. It was a pleasant tree-lined park, with a long sidewalk leading to a children's' playground at the other end. The park itself was a square bounded by war-time houses, most of them freshly painted. The yards were well-kept.

Jed gathered berries, stopping to taste some now and then. The grizzly reared on her hind legs and began to sniff the air. She sensed danger. The silver hairs stood up on the top of her broad back. She heard a sound on the other side of the clearing. She would have to protect her cubs . . .

We walked quickly to the western end of the sidewalk, and then started back to the eastern end of the Park. We had done it, walked through enemy territory! We decided we could celebrate with our picnic. We sat on a bench and began our sandwiches.

"After we finish our lunch we can ask someone where Sasha Churchenko lives. I know it's somewhere near," I said. Hughie and I were so intent on our food that we didn't see them come through the trees.

Jed had an old fur trapper's instinct that he was being stalked, that he was being watched. He quickly took his Green River knife from his belt and whirled round . . .

Six of them, a few years older than us. All in jeans and flannel lumberjack shirts. Ducktail haircuts which our mothers wouldn't let us have. They sneered, then spoke to each other in a language Hughie and I didn't understand. The biggest, clearly the leader, spoke to us in English.

"I'm Leshy Darko and this is my gang. What are you doing in *our* park?"

I looked at Hughie. I spat a bread crust out of my mouth.

"We . . . we were looking for a girl named Sasha Churchenko.

We have something to give her. Do you know where she lives?"

Darko laughed.

"You little shitasses don't have much to give a girl. Tell you what. You give us what you wanted to give her and we'll make sure she gets it, won't we boys?" They all sniggered.

I gave him the chocolate.

"Safe with us," Darko said as he unwrapped the chocolate and threw the foil and paper to the ground. He divided the chocolate up and they ate it.

"Nice chocolate. We'll tell Sasha it tasted great. By the way, little shitfaces, pick up that litter. We don't like litter in our park" I picked the litter up and put it in our Tupperware box. I put the Tupperware back in Hughie's pack. Hughie was shivering with fear.

"Anyway, you turds are lucky. We'll let you go home, East. You're not tough enough to come West. Go home and grow up."

Hughie began to sprint, the only time I had ever seen him run.

"I said WALK," shouted Darko, but Hughie had already disappeared out of the park and over the tracks.

"Your chickenshit friend has more sense than you. Boys,- initiation time."

Two of them pinned my arms behind my back and began to frogmarch me to the train tracks. When I struggled, two others grabbed my legs. Darko and the other boy were at the slough, cutting willows with a pocket knife.

Jed spun round with his knife, but he never got to use it. The grizzly swatted him with her paw, knocking him to the ground. He passed out, briefly coming to only as she ripped the flesh from his leg, feeding it to her nearby cubs . . .

I'll never forget my terror at what happened next. Darko and the others held me even more tightly.

"Andrewchuk, tie him to the tracks."

Using the willows, they tied my hands behind me, and then tied my ankles. They toppled me onto the tracks, tying me to the rails. Darko's eyes narrowed as he squinted at his watch.

"Next train comes in seven minutes. Ever put coins on the tracks, punk? That's what you'll look like." Then they vanished beyond the canal, into Korolenko Park.

Tears welled up in my eyes. I couldn't move. I thought of my mother's warnings, of all the stories we had heard about going west, west of the tracks. I was going to die. But at the same time, a great peace came over me. Grey clouds floated overhead. Redwings sang from the slough, their syrup warbles reminding me of happy visits to my Uncle Jack's wheat farm.

When Broken Hand found his friend Jed, the old trapper's face had been peeled to the skull. Great slices of his arm and leg were missing, boiling up with maggots. Broken Hand took a large needle from his saddlebag and cut some of Jed's buckskin fringes for thread and began to stitch the old man's face together so he'd at least look good for his burial . . .

In that calm, a great strength came over me. I easily pulled free from the willows at my hands, then used a sharp stone to hack through the ones binding my feet. I heard a train in the distance, possibly on another line. I jumped up.

Jed stirred. Hey man, watch out with that needle! You could wound a man! Just sew me up and let's get the hell outta here.

I never knew if Darko knew I would free myself so easily. I later heard others admit to the same humiliating initiation but we had never heard of anyone actually being run over. Probably, Darko would know the exact times when the trains came and plan his ritual accordingly, knowing the victim would escape in a matter of seconds. Or else Darko and his gang would actually cut their prisoner free at the last minute.

Hughie avoided me for a while but we soon renewed our friendship. Sasha came back to play and we all forgot about the tree episode. We gave her some chocolate. I soon moved to another part of the city and never returned to the neighbourhood around Korolenko Park.

I did meet Darko indirectly. Many years later, after a divorce, I began to date a Ukrainian girl named Marisha who had grown up not far from Korolenko Park, though she was born in Odessa. I was in poor health and had lost a lot of weight through illness and worry. Marisha fed me up on Schi, Kapusta, Bliny and Pirozhki. Her house did smell of cabbage, a familiar and now welcome smell. I asked her once if she had ever known a kid named Leshy Darko.

"Everybody knew Leshy. He was a neighbourhood hero and icon. The last I heard, he was working as a roustabout on the oil pipeline way out west somewhere. Alberta I think. Said he really liked the West, likes the wide open spaces. Says he would never come back East again. Needs his freedom, does Leshy."

Marisha laughed. Dogs barked. A train rumbled past.

Tapwa

My two dead great-aunts, Margaret (Maggie) and Jean (*never* Jeannie), came breathless to me in a dream last night saying both the Royal Canadian Mounted Police and the FBI were still after them, but if I could write their story up once and for all, it might finally put an end to the chase and give them some peace. In some grey parallel universe, they are still on the run. I must give them shelter, the same as they were going to give my two brothers and myself (Mark) long ago, when they were living in this world and not their dream one.

Maggie told me just before she died a few years ago that had my mother Elizabeth not survived her cancer treatment, she and Jean would have come up to Canada and kidnapped us, raising us as her own children in New York City. I know she could have done it. It might have been something like this . . .

First. Maggie, tall and bird-like, a sweet sidelong grin, if a bird, then maybe a heron but as active as a wee songbird. An Orkney girl whose father was a joiner on a Shetland whaler. Maggie remembering the long Orkney nights and the long winters too and boatloads of old people taken quietly to Aberdeen to be cured of the "Orkney Melancholia," an old name for what happens when people are hammered by constant dark, rain and wind. One reason they moved to Leith during the Depression was Jimmy her father could find some joinery work there. And there young Maggie managed to read every book in the Macdonald Road Library. For career selection she said "book-keeper" thinking "librarianship" but learned shorthand at the business college before she realised too late that book-keeping was something entirely different. Along with her out-of-work husband and two young children, she took a boat to New York City, living for a time in the Bronx then settling further down in Manhattan, near Central Park, at a time when ordinary folk could afford to live there. Maggie never worried: "After all, I could have stayed in Orkney where there is a millionaire behind every tree," but I never understood the joke until I saw treeless Orkney many years later. The first *skirlie* and *stovies* eaten in a neighbourhood of Puerto Ricans and Haitians, where a woman who could cook tripe like my auntie could was held in high regard.

Spinster Jean, built into Edinburgh with the cobbles, suspicious of any country not having a King and Queen, squat in deep purple wool, her shape that of a postage stamp, her square jaws working on sweets like Berwick Cockles, Hawick Balls, Pan Drops. She was bearer to us in Canada (a country more to her liking) of *The Sunday Post* and Christmas Annuals of "The Broons," "Nero and Zero," "Oor Wullie" and the first Cadbury Chocolate ever tasted on our street. The two aunties smelled of lavender — there was no other smell for aunties in those days.

Jean came to New York often.

"I suppose it's not too bad, living without the monarchy, and your streets are cleaner now."

"Ach, away Jean. Edinburgh was clarty too, buildings black with soot and the rain Jean, mind the rain."

"Ach well, these foreigners, some don't even mind the Queen's English."

"Aye, foreigners like us Jean. *E pluribus unum*, 'out of many one.' That's America and it's no been bad to Sandy and myself. Have a Soor Plum Jean?" Jean would have the hard sweetie. Out would come the false teeth which she then placed in a glass Maggie had already provided for the purpose. Jean gently snoring, dreaming maybe of Yorkshire pudding or the clapshot and stovies to come, while up in the Bronx the baseball Yankees were winning as usual, Whitey Ford twirling a shutout and Mickey Mantle homering over the short right field fence. Maggie never visited Scotland again. Her children grew up in New York City and would live nowhere else while Maggie's husband Sandy was well-matched to his job and social life. More to the point, Maggie could have been happy and self-contained on the moon. It was her Orkney way of things.

Jean sucking on boiled sweets and Maggie buying tripe from the Jamaicans and so it would have gone on, until the letter from my widowed mum Elizabeth, their favourite niece. She was down with cancer again, with the three lads, just bairns, aged ten, eight (me) and six. Older relatives scattered across Canada and none able to care for three of us and most too elderly to take any of us. A Provincial Orphanage it would have to be. Not nice places, something out of Oliver Twist, to mould you into good uncuddled sons of Empire who should be grateful for both parents dying young.

I conjure up those aunts arguing, plotting long into a New York City night, police and ambulance sirens in a city that never awoke because it never slept, except the winos under the bushes in Central Park that Maggie sometimes gave fresh bread to early in the morning.

Jean's vision: us in shorts, school blazers and ties, knees knocking blue from the cold Edinburgh East Wind.

Maggie: taking us on the subway (invented by an Orkney man, so it was) up to the Bronx to watch the Yankees or maybe down to the Battery for an ice cream, whilst growing fat and happy on Scotch pies and cock-a-leekie soup, and we'd probably even eat the tripe just to please her though my younger brother Matt would refuse it, saying it looked like tapeworms.

Maggie's husband Sandy of course had to be kept in the dark about their plot. "Jean, his heart's no all that strong." I could imagine it, Sandy a practical wee Scot, bald head down in the Protestant work ethic, working himself into a lather:

"Margaret, kidnapping across *state*, let alone, *national* boundaries is a capital offence, punishable by electric chair or life imprisonment in a Federal Penitentiary, along with serial rapists, mass murderers and traitors. High Security Prisons!"

So they didn't tell Sandy.

"Sandy, sweetheart, that's us away up to Canada on the Greyhound Bus to see wee Lizzie. Meals in the freezer, shirts all laundered, cheeri-bye."

Sandy, eyes shining, handing over some money, raising a grey eyebrow at Jean, but thinking of some great fly fishing upstate and maybe a Yankee doubleheader and a few beers at O'Hara's. (Maggie was teetotal)

And the two women, one a tall grey grinning bird and the other a purple postage stamp in a pair of sandals and white socks. Jean carrying leather suitcases of a type not seen in New York since before the war (The First One!)

CUT, TO CANADA

Oh Canada, my home and native land . . . with glowing hearts we see thee rise, the True North strong and free . . .

So there we were in Winnipeg on Volcano Avenue, surrounded by Ukrainian children blonder than snow. Icelandic girls named Hecla; Jewish bakeries and drunken Finns and French-speaking boys who fought like wasps. Winters when shirts and trousers froze into blocks on the washing lines while we dreamed of perfect ice, of playing on the wing for Montreal or the Maple Leafs, the Bruins or Blackhawks. Those last two were hockey teams full of Canadians down in America.

America? We'd never been to Maggie's though mum had.

America? Oranges, alligators, skyscrapers, gangsters, Elvis Presley and Davy Crockett and cousins who said *ain't* because they had no Queen to instruct them better, to set a good example.

The aunties would have sucked on sweets and argued a bit, maybe a bit cranky by the time they arrived and not having time to get powdered and lavendered up but straight into the plot. In the dream those two have to come to fetch us and they better have a good excuse.

"Mrs . . . Mrs. Andrewchuk? I'm Elizabeth's aunt Margaret Inkster from New York City and this is her other Aunt, Jean Douglas from Edinburgh . . ."

"The capital of Scotland," interjects Jean.

Mrs. Andrewchuk smells of cabbage and Ukrainian pancakes-*bliny*-which she has been rolling out on a floured board. She has eyes that bore through lies and excuses but she sees only two Old World dears standing in front of her. She whistles us boys down. We get powdery lavendered hugs. "Bairns, I've just told Mrs. Andrewchuk that we'll go off to Assiniboine Park for a wee play before your tea time."

They know our mum is having tests in a city hospital which will require more cancer treatment. Maggie knows these things and is rarely wrong. The *truth of the blood*, she calls it, besides Maggie could read tea leaves and she never told Elizabeth what she read in the teacups one New York day a few months before. She could be wrong, but.

On to Assiniboine Park among the pigeons and gentle old Cree Men, long grey hair braided down their backs, shooting dice and drinking, joking in Cree, dreaming in the September sun of caribou and northern traplines.

The aunties have a real problem here, not helped by the fact they can't drive a car and must get down to the USA border at North Dakota as quickly as possible, before Ma Andrewchuk raises the alarm when they don't come back from Assiniboine Park in an hour or so. Somehow, ladies, you have to get through Customs.

(Brief digression, but pertinent when discussing The USA/Canadian Border. Dreaming an easy Customs route is not possible. Some real border incidents keep intruding into my creativity . . .)

She was American, trying to come into Canada through Montana. She was tall and dark, black hair, patched blue jeans, Indian blouse, no bra, two tattoos, one on each shoulder — a butterfly and a coiled rattlesnake. No messin.

"That fuckin flannel-shirted Canuck bastard of a husband of mine . . . you fuckers let me in so I can tear him a new asshole and when I'm done with him he may be shot at and MISSED but sure as hell shit at and HIT. He's fuckin lower than whale shit and that's on the bottom of the ocean. The only difference between him and a bucket of shit . . . is the bucket!" And so on.

My Canadian pal reckoned they wouldn't let her in just because she swore and that is not the done thing, for a woman to swear in Canada.

Dream intrusions, continued.

My Uncle Larry fell in love with a Ukrainian girl who ran off with a Cajun from Louisiana. He took his anger out on the whole USA:

"The Excited States of Amnesia"

"Yankees are Wankees"

"Sweet Land of Sweet Fuck All"

"Wolves. Kill all theirs so take ours. Their symbol, the Bald Eagle. Kill all theirs so steal ours. Canada the 51st state. America farts, we have to smell it." All because Helga Sawchuk had hair like wheat and eyes like prairie cornflowers.

The Border, handy for outlaws, killers, draft dodgers and rebels but very difficult for two Scottish pensioners with three hungry boys in tow.

Yes, I know it's not Canadian Customs that will be the trouble — it will be American Customs because that's where they're headed but the Canadian authorities will have told their American colleagues to be on the lookout for two elderly Scottish women with three boys who stand together like stair steps, who could fit together like Russian dolls. Canadian Customs have no sympathy for people wishing to leave Canada for America, or kidnapping wee Canadian nationals, definitely not the done thing, it smacks of anarchy (republicanism, same low thing).

It would never work so I dreamed up another Border scene, for in dreams Borders are more fluid and shifting. The Cypress Hills it will have to be.

Go down into Saskatchewan, where eons ago Glaciers came to rest. There is a patch of wildness where the flora and fauna have gone crazy: scorpions, vipers, horned toads, antelopes and a place where whisky runners, wolf hunters, dying buffalo and finally, Sitting Bull, sought refuge. It's a refuge all right. The women and the three boys will be cold, tired and hungry and will be frightened to go into a land of scorpions, vipers and outlaws. So I will dream some earlier summer flowers for them all. Stretching to the Montana Border. Gaillardias, blue fax, wild sunflowers, wild pinks, yellow sweet clover, amethyst asters. The tall grass will undulate like the sea, making the old women feel back home in Scotland. The peaceful scene will soothe us boys for now:

My younger brother Matt. A dark thumb print of a face, scowling and smoky, inscrutable, amenable.

Me: Mark. Eyes too deep in my head, changing colours like chameleons, eyes ringed around the irises like wolf eyes. Volatile.

Older brother: Luke. Just a smiling kid who will adapt to anything and win through. There is no tension in him. Untroubled. A natural leader.

And we gaze to the south Border, lost in more grass and hills, and the sun is going down and it is a bit cooler, the grass is singing to us, with wind and fiddling grasshoppers. Maggie holding hands with Matt who is holding hands with Luke, then me, then Jean. Then to our left, we see the rider, the parting of the tall grass and closer, we see an old Indian, like a Cree in Assiniboine Park. He has long grey hair, let loose now, blowing out behind him like angel wings and his horse is a proud Appaloosa, and he leads two smaller ponies behind. He stops before us, all the horses nervously pawing the ground. Maggie steps forward

Tan sa a se a yum me yun? She asks.
What language do you speak?
Ke mush a gom un.
Cree.
Maggie grins that sidelong grin.
Tan-se-a sin ne ka soo yun?
What is your name?
He answers in Cree.
His name is Michael she says, like the Archangel.
She says in Cree who we are and it sounds like the wind talking.

37

Of course Maggie can speak Cree, her people are Orcadian who worked for the Hudson's Bay company and many of the men took Cree wives and spoke Cree and took the language back to Orkney with them.

Cree Michael helps Maggie and Jean onto one pony. Then my two brothers are lifted onto the other, and I mount behind Michael, hanging onto his long grey hair. He pauses, motions the others in front of him. He asks Maggie:

Tapwa? (Yes?)

Maggie looks around at all of us and grins. "**Tapwa? Aye, Tapwa.**"

And we ride into the dying sun and late summer flowers, the grasshoppers fiddling our way South, where we will be together forever in our dreams. Where we will all find peace.

All of It

"My own mother and father died in the Great Hunger in County Clare. I do not like to see any creature go hungry. So, I fed it to the dogs. All of it."

Tim's Pat's Mickeen, to a Yale zoologist, 1878

Tim's Pat's Mickeen "fed his dreams to the dogs" is all anybody said about the man in the photo on my mantelpiece. The man in the faded rust-coloured photo leans against a wooden boat shed somewhere in Newfoundland in the last century. At least a dozen dogs are snapping at his heels. Mickeen peers from under heavy tired eyelids, almost hiding and indifferent to the canine chaos all around him. He is holding something in his large hands that looks like a curved wooden tool. This thing is the very reason this long-dead man should be in the *Guinness Book of Records*. This thing is all that was left after the lean hounds had eaten the beast it came from.

I care about Mickeen, my great-grandfather's brother. My eyes are exactly like his and I too have much more time for dogs than people. And I too have fed my own dreams to the dogs — —for I used to write fiction until clever critics sunk their fangs into it. I write only non-fiction now. I've been gathering a few facts about Mickeen's strange life. Mickeen vanished in 1906, in San Francisco, on his way to China. He wrote his last note, in English, to my grandmother. The note was lost but said:

"I am going West one last time, where the sun will be setting."

Yours I remain, Mickeen.
San Francisco, 1906.

My goal now is to get Mickeen down off the mantelpiece into the *Guinness Book of Records*, for capturing a sea monster, single-handed.

****

Mickeen was starving barefoot in County Clare, fourteen years old and tiptoeing over typhus and cholera. He wasn't able to buy a passage across the Ocean so he stowed away in the hold of a timber ship returning to Newfoundland. Arriving in Canada, he was pulled out of the hold, wrapped in his own bloody vomit from his guts being ripped by ill-ground Indian meal. O'Hanlon, a local potato merchant, asked him in Irish his story and Mickeen, later fed and healthy said he was an orphan; his parents and five of six brothers had died in a shallow ditch. My great grandfather who came to Canada (many years after Mickeen) was that other living brother. They never saw each other again.

*   *   *

As far as I know, Mickeen never talked to Charles Darwin. Darwin would have found him good craic but the scientist would have had to learn West Clare Irish to enable Mickeen to put him right on a few points about natural selection and giantism. The story is older than both Mickeen and Darwin, in languages neither of them would understand. Myths. Poems. Ship's logs. Here are some facts:

The octopus has eight tentacles. The squid has ten; eight normal ones and two extra long ones for catching and holding prey. Forget the gentle octopus for now, a small retiring creature. Not so the squid. A streamlined aggressive meat eater. They are mollusks, related to snails; "cephalopods" because their heads have feet attached. Common squid are small and delicious to eat. But, since the time of Homer, giant squid have been reported as doing the eating, natural to a creature hundreds of feet long and weighing several tonnes! The reality of these giant squid later became a scientific problem. New England sea captains, tea merchants and squid-jiggers had regularly seen these monsters and duly reported them to scientists and professors who supped their claret and said "tsssk, tssk, these childish jack tars most certainly have vivid imaginations. Do they not comprehend that nature does not throw up freaks, but rather selects fastidiously those balanced and familiar species which we everywhere know from scientific analysis rather than primitive fancy?"

Tssk. Tssk.

Man was basking in the Age of Reason and Rationality, so much so that when a French ship had a real tussle with a giant squid off the coast of West Africa and brought back a huge chunk of it for inspection, a scientist in the French Academy of Science argued that the men had done battle with a piece of sea weed, concluding:

"This will suffice, I think, to persuade the wise and especially, the man of science, not to admit into the catalogue those stories which mention extraordinary creatures like the sea serpent and the giant squid, the existence of which would be some sort of contradiction of the great laws of harmony and equilibrium which have sovereign rule over living nature as well as senseless and inert matter."

All this while Mickeen was living in a wooden shack near the sea in an isolated cove in Newfoundland where all the lean hounds of the area gathered because they sensed that a man who knew so much about starvation would feed them; Mickeen snored happily in his hard bed while:

In Pimlico, in clubs of marble and dark carved wood, with shelves slumbering in vellum underneath maps in Latin and Greek, and the finest claret being served with the driest gin, twirled by tongues confident in speaking a scientific "truth" that was a lie because it did not take account of dreams and nightmares; because it did not fish for cod off the hard Newfoundland coast; because it did not know facts came in all sizes. BIG FACTS were slithering in deep waters.

By the time Mickeen was making some living from codfish, unknown to the smug naturalists of Greater London, huge creatures scientists said were hallucinations or nightmares or brandy-inspired dreams were dying off the coasts of Newfoundland and Labrador. These mollusks were: sixty or more feet long, with tentacles a further thirty five feet, eyes as big as dinner plates, belonging to predators much bigger than the small boats floating around their dead or dying bodies. Trouble was, squids are soft-bodied and deteriorate quickly so by the time-learned men got there from Boston or New York, there was nothing left that crows, foxes, gulls and sharp rocks hadn't destroyed. It was a mass suicide, never really understood; perhaps changes in water temperature, food shortage, navigation errors and so on. Fishermen and their sons were going out from Thimble Tickle, Catalina, Bona Vista, Great Bell Island, Logie Bay to witness this great dying, so common to them that they didn't understand what the professors and zoologists were fussing about.

"Giant Squid? *Mon pere*, a fact of life here."

But *some* of the squid were not dead when the fishermen found them.

Was it not Theophile Piccot and his son Thomas, who found a monster squid thrashing in the sea near Great Bell Island and hacked one of its huge tentacles off with an axe and had it measured; a squid sixty feet long, five feet across, tentacles thirty feet or more; both men with a Gallic shrug said it was small compared to what that crazy Irishman had captured down the coast. It became known in all the small fishing hamlets of Eastern Newfoundland that no squid yet found or even imagined was like that of the Irishman, Mickeen, who it was said simply fed it to his pack of hounds.

*   *   *   *

In French, Gaelic, Irish and English the story differed yet agreed; no one had actually seen the monster but had all heard how it came to be.

Mickeen rowed out on a calm day in October, around the rocky point towards a place heaving with cod when he saw the beast floating on the sea, long arms undulating in the current. Mickeen was not pleased that it was gorging itself with the very codfish that Mickeen himself ate or sold or fed to his dogs; great luscious white fish, shining in the sun — fish of great beauty and sweetness.

Mickeen, eyes always nearly closed with sleep or tiredness, took time to wonder at the size of the evil eye, the largest eye of any living creature and it was the eye, a fishermen learned from Mickeen later, that made Mickeen want to kill the creature — that unblinking devil's eye, or maybe, it was the bulk of the beast that made Mickeen think his dog food worries would be over for a long time, for he was fishing longer and longer hours just to get enough for his beloved pets — the "loves of his heart" he called them.

Maybe it was a foolish thing Mickeen did next, for the creature was happy to keep feeding, not even aware of the tired man in the twenty-foot boat made of good Newfie larch; the large luminous eye saw only the boiling backs of golden cod. Mickeen sunk a grapnel hook deep into the eye and I could imagine the sea boiling and billowing, almost sucking the small boat down. Then, the creature sounded, and Mickeen was towed by the short grapnel rope (which he managed to tie to a larger rope in the boat). Next, Mickeen poised over the green whirlpool, hand on axe (every Newfoundland fisherman in those days took a sharp axe on board — why? To cut off tentacles as big around as a fisherman's waist from creatures whose existence had not yet been granted by famous scholars in London) but the rope went

42

slack for a moment and the creature surfaced just in front of Mickeen's boat and headed for Ireland; some fishermen recalled Mickeen going past, holding onto his rope, corncob pipe spluttering smoke and they shouted in French and in Irish but Mickeen smiled and shook his head **NO** and they knew it was then between Mickeen and what was on the end of his line — Mickeen towed by a nightmare or a dream . . .

*   *   *   *   *   *

I can't imagine it, the horror of it, being towed over the open sea by a sea troll, many times larger than your own beautiful human-made boat; the loneliness under the moon, on the cold October salt; one Frenchman who later spoke to Mickeen said the Irishman slept much of the time, saying "having survived the Famine and The Fever, what is this fat snail to me but a thing to feed the hounds and besides, I can cut the rope at any time, man, at any time at all." He didn't cut the rope though.

All night on this mysterious sleigh ride, then a great whoosh of water and the animal headed for shore, for Newfoundland in a great turning arc under the soft moon. And in the long night the monster followed the coastline and Mickeen could see the lonely lights of the fishermen's cabins. Then the rope went slack. Daylight came. Mickeen knew the place well, not very far from his own wooden hut and not far from his yelping hungry dogs. Mickeen told someone he could not see what was on the end of his line until he felt the rope go slack. On a sea as calm as glass, the squid floated to the surface. It was the colour of rust — and it was dead. Mickeen gave out one sharp flash of breath while his pipe dropped sizzling into the sea. He could not believe the size of the monster and shuddered at his foolishness. No other man saw Mickeen then and what was on the end of his rope and no man ever saw it after the tides pushed it shoreward and into a rock cleft and Mickeen, seeing the great flock of gulls and all the coarse hungry foxes of Newfoundland, whistled loud from his teeth and his hounds came running into the shallow sea, nipping chunks from the great squid. They feasted for days but no men came, because the other fishermen were up in Labrador looking for an Irishman being towed to Ireland. Most were probably expecting to find only the splintered larch of his fine boat.

Then a great storm came and battered what was left of the beast into salt-laden smithereens.

*   *   *   *

It was about this time that a brave fisherman named Stephen Sperring and two other men captured a big squid at Thimble

Tickle Bay, the largest squid ever officially measured and recorded. Its body was twenty feet, its tentacles thirty-five feet long and as thick as a man's body. Its eye was 18 inches across and a professor estimated its weight at as much as thirty tonnes. It is the squid in the *Guinness Book of Records*—the largest ever caught.

*   *   *   *

Maybe, we only have Mickeen's word for the size of his own squid. Mickeen—who feigned total ignorance of English when a Quaker professor from Yale named Nimrod Patience came to interview him. Nimrod, legend has it, asked him how big the creature was, quoting the dimensions of the squid Stephen Sperring caught. Mickeen only laughed and said in broken English **"you can ask my dogs."** But Mickeen did show the Professor one thing of interest, the thing in the photograph like a curved shoehorn. It was the "beak" of the squid. Squid have beaks something like a parrot's which often are the only things surviving decomposition. Mickeen had saved it as a souvenir. He let the professor touch, measure and photograph it—the photograph on the mantelpiece. It seems parts of squids have such a perfect geometrical ratio and proportion that accurate guesses of the animal's total size can be made from these small clues. Professor Patience measured the beak at 24 inches diameter. The Guinness Book of Records squid had a beak nine inches in diameter! Patience said Mickeen's squid would thus be about three times the size of the record squid, minimum!

Professor Patience went back to his University, sent the photo to Mickeen then died shortly afterwards.

Mickeen wandered further west, to the wheat fields of Manitoba, then to the lumber camps of the Yukon, with some gold panning on the way.

*   *   *

I'm not happy with any of this. Mickeen taking his great nightmare on the sea with him to the San Francisco earthquake, a Professor's premature death robbing him of some fame or even fortune. I could let it all go I suppose; after all, it happened a long time ago. But I can't let it go. Somebody once said a sated man has *dreams,* a starving man has *nightmares.* Until I learn the truth of his hungry life, I must feed off nightmares. I am not yet sated.

Long Line Rider

Jimmy, who is now dead, was in a sleeping bag on the floor. The motel room had two single beds, I in one, Jackman in the other. Drawing the short straw, Jimmy got the floor. A cheap motel, on the way to Seattle for Christmas. A blizzard. "Christ, my car has disappeared under snow," says Jackman, drawing the curtains. He lights a Marlboro, passes the pack to Jimmy. No food. Only three beers, one for each of us. Fifty miles to Seattle and we can't move. The motel neon looks pale and faraway, like the face of a sinking man.

Jimmy draws on the cigarette, drawls. *"Christ the world is all afloat and life preservers there are none."* Some poet or other and Jimmy knows them all, even in French. There is still electricity for the time being. Jackman turns on the TV. It works.

It is a talk show and there is music. It is 1969. None of us are really watching, just listening to the wind and snow outside. On screen, a man sings. Immediately we listen. We really hear the words. We feel this is a song being sung against the odds in New York while we are in a blizzard on the way to Seattle. The song is about some prison in Arkansas where they kill then bury inmates who have no record or identity. As if they never existed. The singer. Bobby Darin, not the former clean-cut pop singer but bearded, gaunt, intense. Different. We are listening, forgetting the blizzard, the motel. We are only hearing the words and are held by them. "Christ," we all say at once, in Trinity. "Did you hear that?"

Jimmy's fag is held mid-air. Jackman spilled some of his beer when we heard the lyric.

"The ground coughs up some roots, wearin' denim shirts and boots."

"Christ," says Jackman.

The singer finishes. *"Long Line Rider, haul em away... USA."* The audience hesitates, then applauds.

Then the power goes. The black TV screen sinks into its own black hole. Everywhere lights have all gone out. The wind is all we hear above our own beating hearts.

Dreaming Babel

Isaak Emmanuilovich Babel had been dead twenty-seven years when I first met him in Moscow in 1968. I was 18. I am now 47 (the same age Babel was when last seen alive).

* * *

Moscow, Idaho, Western USA that is.

I was a student, supposedly studying petrochemical rock formations and the geology of undersea oil deposits. I lived in a wind-riven wooden house with several other students. The big house faced a tree-covered park, several blocks square. There were benches under the trees. I went to the benches to escape piles of unwashed dishes, loud stereos and arguments about revolution (for we all agreed that revolution or counter-revolution was coming.)

The park had no real reason for being there since all the houses nearby already had big gardens and front lawns, full of wisteria or shrubs native to Scandinavia and Northern Europe, where most of the town founders came from a century or more before. One part of the park never changed. Near its western rim, was a row of tall fir trees. Through all the seasons, the evergreens changed colours only subtly, from lime to deep blue. There were hardwood trees too and in autumn, the bright dead leaves swirled and rustled around the park, under the benches and around your feet. Squirrels would gather pine cones, sniff the benches, then scurry away. From any corner of the park, you saw snow-covered mountains. Local children played in the park, riding bikes, sledding, throwing snowballs. Many of them, dressed in thick parkas and fur boots, were blonder than snow. I only remember the children in snow because I was rarely in the park in summer, the only season sure to be free of snow. It bothers me too that I never learned the names of the hardwood trees. I vividly remember the Douglas Fir trees - maybe just because I knew their names. The other trees just fade away when I try to recall them.

* * * *

I met Babel in Moscow, this way. I went to a lecture by locally-born Katinka Ivanovich, a teacher of Russian.

"Babel (she said it BAH byeel) was an outsider, a Jewish intellectual from Odessa who rode out with the Red Cavalry, on Gorki's advice, to gather experience of real life in order to improve his short story writing. Isaak Babel described that brutal life with clarity and fairness, but always as an outsider. His stories had great appeal at the time, but they later got him into trouble with Stalin." "What happened to Babel?"

"Nobody knows. He vanished in one of Stalin's purges. Many think Stalin killed as many Jews as Hitler did. All the books mention him 1894/7-1939? or circa 1941. Russia was being attacked by Hitler, and hundreds of thousands of Russians were starving. Maybe Babel just disappeared with the rest, into a mass grave. His works were proscribed, but revived after Stalin's death."

She described how Babel took the reader into the sights, aromas and intrigues of the Odessa ghetto; its Rabbis, gangsters, dock workers.

I went to the library but his name was missing from every collection of Russian short stories. I went to Katinka Ivanovich's office but she laughed when I told her. "Babel has truly vanished, the world over. He was only recently translated into English. Here. Take this 'Odesskiye Rasskazy' with English translation. Keep it as long as you wish."

"Thank you," I said in Russian. She grinned.

* * * *

Odessa is a dark dancer, in bright blue skirt, white blouse. She dances to the old Jewish music of the ghetto. Under her skirt are great red petticoats, rustling and sometimes sticking to her dark sweating thighs. She is barefoot and leaps onto the tables, inviting all to shelter under her red petticoats. Many go under, eagerly, except one dark shy boy with glasses. He is in the corner writing nervously. He would like to go under the petticoat, he is throbbing for it but he fears the heady perfume there, he fears he would pass out under its fragrance, then never wake up . . .

So, he stays in the corner, writing, watching, blushing. Stepping near the dancer but always out of reach of her dizzying skirts.

* * * *

Me. Why Babel? Babel was the outsider who did not feel superior to the cruel laughing cavalrymen who killed, loved and laughed. He felt inferior to them. I know the feeling.

I, Michael Klein.

My father was Jewish, but not an intellectual, a doctor or professor. He was a stevedore on the docks in Portland, Oregon.

He was never a practising Jew and I myself knew nothing about religion. My old man, David, was a kind of working-class intellectual. He had a huge wall chart up in our bathroom. It had all the bones of the human body highlighted. He broke so many bones while working on the waterfront that he labelled each one on the chart: "Metacarpal, broken, June 1967 unloading bananas from Ecuador." I thought he was trying to break every bone in his body before he died. Then, I suppose, he would just vanish into the wall chart. I am dark, thin, short, and wear glasses: a city boy in an agricultural town where everyone seems tall and blonde. In truth, the people here are friendly and I have no reason to feel so cut off from them.

Why Babel? Remember, this is 1968, Paris, Chicago, Prague. The whole world is erupting and there is nowhere safe. You can feel it in the air. The Cossacks are coming. The Czars of the world are frightened. They are sending out the troops. I had trouble concentrating on petrochemicals when I could almost hear the clatter of horse hooves coming through the park.

Portland was just like Odessa. Awash with Russians and Africans. Its Burnside Avenue full of hordes of hobos just off the western boxcars, wintering over in the city, a wet but warmer place. Street preachers, great black men in turbans, cowboys, Indians, Chinese, Vietnamese, sailors, drifters. Something always faintly sinister and apocalyptic about Burnside Avenue. For me, it was an easy dream-shift to Odessa: Babel and I are soaking it up. The rich aroma of wheat, sugar and wool from the teeming docks. In the ghetto, young violinists are practising the same notes over and over again. Zimbalist. Heifitz. "Jascha, Mein Liebling, keep up the good violin work and you will go all over the world with that music." Babel and I, almost physical twins, duck down alleys, steal from fruit stalls when we are hungry, absorbing stories from fishwives, pimps, sailors, gangsters, but always, one ear cocked to the wind. Maybe you would hear hooves on the cobbles first, or see dust in the distance, or hear guns and whips and harsh guttural cries in other languages. Pogroms and Jew-Dreaming, Babel baiting to keep the unruly elements happy and diverted. Babel and I slip into the corners, with scorpions, until the troops pass. When it is safe, the dancing woman comes out, her red petticoats swirling in the sultry air of Odessa.

* * * *

Odessa seeped into my own Moscow, between the ploughing

and harvesting and oceans of wheat from the great Palouse country. Midnight walks down long streets between pickup trucks, past Country and Western bars and Chinese restaurants, in wind so cold my snot would freeze, and stay frozen, until I could thaw it later with the steam from a coffee mug. Many of the students had been loggers and lumberjacks and took me in tow, out of pity. Johnny Loggins put it bluntly: "It's time you lost your cherry you little runt. I know just the place."

Loggins knew the place. A logging town about thirty miles away. Friday night. Six of us crammed into Loggins' rusted Chevy Impala. The house was a huge three story wooden house in the centre of town. It had a swing on the wrap-around wooden porch. Loggins bounded up the stairs, banged on the doors, and lights came on. We went into the hall. Peacock feathers, stuffed beavers. A mounted grizzly bear head grinned down at me. Loggins shoved me into a room, then they all disappeared. A woman removed my glasses and all I saw then was a bloated dark shape looming over me. Cut. Thanks Loggins, for nuthin. Bang on the door. The rest of the bunch, smirking, grinning. Loggins stuck out a huge hand. "Welcome to manhood, Klein. Yer one of us now."

One of them. I never told Loggins that nothing happened in that room smelling of nicotine, stale beer and makeup. The huge woman merely fell asleep but kept me awake all night with her snoring. Dawn couldn't come fast enough. I walked down the long wooden steps with my own variety of Cossacks. I wish Babel could have been there.

* * * *

My copy of Babel was well-worn and the binding had broken. As a result, the pages were falling out. I took it to Katinka Ivanovich and offered to pay for it but she just shrugged and told me to keep it as I had earned it.

* * * *

I was sitting in the park in late Spring. Last autumn's fallen leaves from the hardwoods blew across the park, now noisy with children's laughter and birdsong. Sun reached the ground, coming through in biblical shafts. Reading Babel, I was hardly aware of someone sitting on the far end of my bench.

"Babel? I like him too."

I looked up. Christine Olaffson. I knew her but we had never spoken. I stuttered.

"He . . . hello. Are you studying Russian?"

"No. My mother is good friends with Katinka Ivanovich and Babel is her religion. She passes out his books like Gideon Bibles, but I'm a willing convert."

"You live near here, don't you?"

"I've lived here all my life. My father sells farm machinery. Tell me/they say Babel just vanished, disappeared."

"Nobody really knows," I said.

"It is the outsider in Babel I identify with. Babel never belonged anywhere. In the ghetto. In the army. The Revolution. The Soviet.Maybe he just walked away from it all." When Christine said "walked away from it all" she rubbed her foot through the dead leaves.

"I don't think so. Katinka Ivanovich says there are now papers which proved Babel died in a concentration camp. Anyway, you're not an outsider. You're part of the town."

She laughed. "You mean, I'm tall, blonde and Swedish Lutheran? You can live in a place all your life and never feel part of it. My mother was born in Sweden but left her village when she was ten. We visited a few

years ago. My mother couldn't remember much and felt a totaloutsider. I fit right in and was speaking Swedish in a week. I felt as though I had gone home, not my mother."

She got up to go.

"I'll see you again. The Isaak Babel Restoration Society."

She laughed and waved, disappearing down the long dark tunnel of fir trees.

I went to the park the next few days but Christine wasn't there. Then, it was time for me to go back to Portland for the summer.

* * * *

I remembered a strange thing though. The first time I had ever really noticed Christine Olaffson was one Spring day in the park, a few years before. She had on one of these billowing floral peasant dresses. The wind blew and I could see her petticoats swirling. They were red.

* * * *

I returned to the park and town on a golden September day. I plucked up courage to knock on Christine's front door. Her mother came to the door.

"Christine worked all summer. The last we've heard, she worked in New York City, on her way to Sweden."

"Thanks," I mumbled.

Trouble was, my old man decided to add to his broken bone collection by dropping a stevedore's hook on his head, breaking his skull in three places. I needed to help out at home so had to drop out of my petrochemical studies, which I must admit, had suffered greatly after I met Babel.

* * * *

I never got to return to that park but I am now the same age as Babel when he went missing. Ah, Babel, the clouds rolled over Odessa, over the dock, over the wool and sugar, the Yiddish and Russian, over and under the petticoats of the brown dancers. The Cossacks never came that final time. No, we never heard their horses.

* * * *

Surely, I could never vanish. Friends and family would miss me. The state has names and numbers for me in their computers. I have my own books, photos, videos. A man could not just vanish today. Could he?

Surely not, it is impossible.

Yet, that park has vanished. The wheat fields and fine Indian ponies are gone. Christine Olaffson is gone and everything will vanish completely when my memories are gone.

And Babel, when this story is written, you too will have vanished into that grey gulag again. Da Svidanya. Farewell.

We leave home.

We seek home.

Then, we truly vanish.

The Tea Boy's Tale

I work in the studio where there is a sign in French that says "This Train Makes No Stops." I make tea. I fetch tobacco. I bring coffee. I clean the studio, taking care not to create more dust than I remove. I go to a local shop for the special paints which The Painter uses. He calls me "Catalan boy" although he calls me by my real name "Jordi" as well. I call him "The Painter" or "Mr. Miro." He pays me in francs which I take home to my aunt and uncle. He pays me far too much but pretends it is the "going rate." Perhaps he feels sorry for me because I am an orphan and do not live in my own country. It is a good job. He is a kind man. He works very hard but so do I. I am not allowed to be in the studio when he is painting but I sometimes steal glances at his work. Most of the days were the same but this one day was different. Very different. The events of that day still haunt me even though I am an old man now. But for that day I would have worked in the studio for many more years.

He always spoke to me in Catalan. "Jordi, go to the shop and fetch some of the blue I like. And the gentian. You know the kind. Put it on my account. Tell Monsieur Le Bris that I will pay him on Thursday as I usually do. Here is some extra money for chocolate for yourself. But don't be long. I have visitors today."

Down the stairs out into the Rue Blomet, which is also the street where I live. The colours of the shop fronts wash together. Pastry shop. Tobacconist. Bookshop. Lingerie. My aunt and uncle live further along the street where the houses are older and smaller.

When I got back to the studio the men were already there. They nodded to me. Sometimes in the past they had given me money or sweets but not today.

Eluard and Arp I had seen before. There were two new people. A German and a Belgian. All painters; or maybe, a poet and a sculptor.

The Painter was cheerful. "Thank you Jordi. We might like some coffee later. And maybe some special cigars. Perhaps it is time for you to go into the store room and begin tidying, carefully."

Carefully because that's where his paintings were stored. The unsold ones. Most were still unsold.

I do not care much for his paintings of ladies with skins like metal but there are some canvases of the Catalan farm and land-scape which are like dreams captured with paint. The warmest yellows and browns, the odd splash of green, red and black. The Painter is good with the blue as well. One painting I like is almost all blue but for a few slivers of black and white, like teardrops on the canvas.

I sometimes weep when I see the painting of the Catalan farm, with its suggestions of lizards and funny water pots and cans. He has the sky perfect. It really is that colour and it is not just blue but a Catalan blue. This is the blue paint he sends me for but he also mixes it until it is perfect before a brush ever touches it. That shade of blue makes me homesick.

In truth, I was not tidying up much but looking at each painting. "Look but don't touch" he smiled but I did what I was told. Like all quiet men who speak sparingly, he really means what little he says. This room is a warm room and winter Paris days I have been in there and felt home again, with the heat that warms from the heart outwards but with a hint of a breeze and a cool drink from the well. I can almost imagine the leathery lizards springing from the canvas.

At first, the voices next door whisper like the feet of mice in the walls.

Each speaks French in his own manner, even the Frenchmen differing in tone and accent from one another. They speak too fast for me to understand every word. I can't quite hear it and don't wish to, because most of it is adult talk.

I peek around the still open door. The men are smoking and drinking. The Painter says little; he is listening. There is much humour there, mostly directed at Mr. Miro.

"Catalan, how can an *accountant* paint so well?"

They wink at one another behind his back.

"We will have some women tonight Painter, do you wish to come with us? Too much work young man . . . it is not good for the . . . " and the man, Eluard, points to his lower parts.

My ears prick up. They are mentioning Real Madrid and I am a Barcelona supporter.

"Hey, Miro, have you heard the latest score? Real Madrid: 2 Surreal Madrid: Pink Giraffes," and they all laugh—even my boss.

The Painter might not know who Real Madrid are but I am of course a Barca man, one of the *culés* of the many Barcelona supporters too poor to buy a ticket but sitting on the rails with their rear ends sticking out. I am proud to be one of the *culés* and I still follow the football scores. I laugh at the joke because it seems to be making fun of Real Madrid and that is a good thing. The Real supporters call us gypsies and thieves but they know we are the better team.

These men admire this Catalan and his hard work but he is not one of them with their drugs, women and drink. While they are out doing those things, The Painter is busy mixing paints or painting.

But I get back to work. I make sure none of the paintings touch each other. I lift the soft cloth covers to let some air reach the canvas but I must make sure the small window curtain is always in the right position to filter out the sunlight. I have a small feather duster which I dab so delicately. I also make sure the wood for the canvas framework is arranged by size and kept neatly stacked, out of the way.

And the voices next door are still soft; still gentle and still laughing. The Painter does not often laugh but I can sometimes hear his laugh too. I am thinking how happy I am and how happy I will be to leave in an hour or so with francs in my pocket. My uncle and aunt are proud of me and I am proud to hand over the money to them for food. It is not a bad life. . .

Then like the sound of mice stopping running in the walls, I hear a change in the musical note of their speech next door: from soft to loud, from kind to cruel. Something next door has gone wrong. I had better look. I swear by my namesake *Saint Jordi* this is what I saw:

My master is sitting in a chair and two of the men have pinned his arms to the side, while a third is slipping a hangman's noose over his head. He is not struggling or speaking though I wish him to. The men are laughing but their laughter is now cruel.

"Speak, bourgeoisie. What do you really think of Fauvism? Give us your opinion. We are beginning to think you imagine yourself superior to us in some way. We are tired of your silence."

Another interrupts:

"Silence is like death. If you wish to be dead we will help you on your way, eh?"

The two men pinning his arms are not smiling.

I look for clues to this thing. It seems real to me but the men are laughing and my ever-serious boss is not protesting. But he is not speaking. I need to stay hidden but I also need to do something. I am not sure why but I think it is important for me to interrupt this.

Now I remember it. Something that has troubled me about that day. It has troubled me for many years. It is *fear*. Until then, there had been no *fear* in the studio.

In his eyes there is fear but how can I explain this? It is not fear of his "friends" or of the noose or what they are saying. I will explain this later, now that I am a grown man, now that the future of that time has become my past.

Regardless of the consequences, I had to save my boss, The Painter, Maestro Miro.

I stumbled into the room shouting

"There is a rat in the storeroom! I fear it will eat Mr. Miro's paintings! Quickly, come. Kill the rat!"

My shout has stopped the men in their tracks. The noose is dropped. They free his arms. My master is clearly angry but perhaps not just at me.

"Boy, how dare you interrupt us? These are important men, my friends, and their time is precious and you come in here talking of rats . . . take these francs and never come back. I demand loyalty and silence . . . Get out! Now!"

I refused his money. I turned quickly for the door so he wouldn't see my tears. I ran down the stairs and out onto the Rue Blomet.

I didn't say to him that *"friends" don't put nooses around your neck.*

That *human rats are more dangerous than real ones.*

That *money wouldn't buy loyalty or silence.* Not from a Catalan.

I've read about this incident later but I am never mentioned. One photographer even did Miro's portrait with a noose in the background. It was all a big joke they say and the books repeat it.

They say the former accountant Miro with his blue business suit and short hair was boring and too conventional to be a revolutionary painter. They didn't understand his hard work. His refusal to take drugs, drink too much or visit brothels seemed to be a criticism of their own bohemian ways. Miro once told me that only his paintings spoke for him and that he had no time for foolishness. Maybe that's why he kept silent with a noose around his neck.

Back to that day: I now understand what I did not understand then. Like Miro I could not put my fear into words. He put his fear into his paintings and I think as his friends clowned around with the noose, he was having a vision which went into his later paintings. He saw a vision of Guernica and Franco, of Hitler and the demise of his Catalan homeland after the Spanish Civil War. He was thinking not of the noose of the present but the noose of the future. He was thinking of a time when friends would kill friends for mere words; for simply giving the wrong answers to difficult questions. He was thinking of the fragility of life at the foot of the hanging tree.

No I didn't save his life nor was his anger solely against me for my childish lie about rats. I had interrupted his vision of the future, made real by his fear of the noose around his neck.

I went home not long afterward. My aunt and uncle could not afford to feed me without the francs I had been bringing home. I lived in the streets for a time, then I was adopted by some distant relatives who were kind to me. I survived the noose of the Civil War and Hitler and all the rest of it, as Miro did. He outlived them all. That day, so long ago, even the train that makes no stops must have at least slowed down.

Red Flyer

The red car has skidded, spinning off the wet Spring road, flipping over three times. Black shiny bits from the car lay strewn on the muddy hill. Rain runs in dark wrinkles over the road. Newborn lambs bleat in the distance. Crows perch on a fence. The car driver is there but also not there. His mind is far away. Red wagon, black bits strewn on a hill.

Three boys a long way from home are walking up a green hill in the middle of America. The hill is at the edge of a town where they may soon be adopted and separated. It is late Spring, nearly summer. They are brothers, aged six, eight and ten, and would fit together like Russian dolls. White T-shirts, faded blue jeans, blonde hair. The hill is steep, covered in grass and clover. In Spring, lovers lie on blankets on the hill. In Summer, the 4th of July fireworks display is arranged on its slopes. In Winter, children take sleds and toboggans down it. At the bottom is a basketball court that is used all day and late into the night. Right up to the hill's edge is the town itself, its red brick streets shaded by maples and yellow poplar.

The boys see green hill, blue sky. To the left are pine plantations. At the very top, between hill and sky is a grove of Osage Orange trees, called "hedge apples" locally. Far to the right is an outdoor swimming pool. At night older boys climb the hill, drink and smoke. They try to throw the huge green Osage fruit into the pool where an early morning lifeguard will fish them out with his long-handled net.

The wagon is shiny red. It was a Christmas present to all three of them. It had a lone red ribbon on the black handle, there under the tree. On the left side, white letters said "Red Flyer." The oldest boy secretly thought it was babyish so never used it much. The other two boys used it for everything, filling it with water to keep turtles and goldfish in, or filling it with pine cones or limestone fossils. It carried baseball gloves and bats, basketballs and footballs in season. The youngest would be pulled self-consciously by either of the other two. The wagon handle is long and black. It tilts back over the wagon and is nearly the wagon's length. It leans at about a 45-degree angle when positioned back. The two oldest boys pull the wagon up the hill, occasionally trading off. The youngest boy is doing enough just to keep walking; yet none of them stop. They talk.

"Should we be doing this?"

"Yeah, we should."

"What if the wagon breaks?"

"It won't break."

"Chicken."

"I'm not."

These boys don't know exactly why they are doing this in front of a sleeping town. In fact, nobody has seen them except the living things on the hill. Fox squirrels, bluejays, cardinals, tiger swallowtail butterflies, hatching cecropia moths.

The boys are determined but trudging too, as if to something painful, final. They couldn't later say why but in three heads all the answers were there.

It was a dead father.

It was a mother with cancer.

It was living with relatives, talk of orphanages.

It was the sound of a freight train waking you at night, moving off, further away until you could hear it no more.

It was winters without deep snow.

It was sleeping four to one small room, two to a bed.

It was the gnawing feeling that a shiny wagon at Christmas would never be enough, that the three of them could never be bought that way.

That their world would never be shiny and new, with clean lettering. For someone else maybe but not for them.

Their gut feeling that this land would never fit them, that they would never fit it.

That they would all three have to take the wagon right to the edge, down the entire slope of the park and right out its gate, heading home.

They needed to say this somehow. This morning they understood but could not say what they understood.

Before we get to that morning we will get to just now.

Now, there are two of the three boys left to think about the red wagon on the hill.

One of the boys, the youngest, just walked off the planet, vanished to all family and friends, off all police reports, missing persons records, just kept walking up a hill (or down), just kept going.

One went somewhere to a war where there were snipers, cobras and more ways to die than anyone has imagined. He went into a jungle and never came out, "missing in action."

But back on the hill, fifty years ago, the three boys are like small blond pilgrims, angels in the Midwest sun, in the sparkling dew. From a distance, only their wagon seems to move. It is glistening, black and red. The boys don't look back to the sleeping town, beyond the giant maples where the day begins, with frying bacon, strong coffee and their own sleeping house where they said they would get up early and go fishing in the nearby pond, an easy, allowable thing for these boys to do.

And they reached the top.

They felt dizzy looking back down and that's when they knew they had chosen the wrong thing to do. The town was tiny, the hill and sky very big. They sat under the Osage Orange tree and listened to jaybirds scolding somewhere, watched big yellow butterflies pulse on the grass and fly away. The boys were thirsty and hot. The oldest one turned the wagon so it would point down hill.

"Hold the wagon," he says, getting in.

Then the middle one climbs in.

The youngest sits in front. The middle boy holds the handle straight up, in front of the face of the youngest and over his head, like an umbrella.

Now, it's all in front of them. The town in morning mist like a jungle settlement. The lonely basketball court, which in a few hours will be crowded. The locked tennis courts next to it. Swimming pool empty, the morning breeze only rippling the chlorinated surface. The leaves of the trees are just barely moving. The sky is increasing each shade of blue, with bright sun above it all.

They hesitate, maybe waiting for an objection, an intervention, maybe an adult to tell them no, not to do it. And they waited in the birdsong of the morning but no intervention came. Like a man in a wheelchair, the eldest started the wagon moving with his arms. The wagon moved with the laughter of the boys, gaining speed.

It then began to shake back and forth, then shake some more. The handle was the problem, hard to grip, harder to hold.

The handle broke free from the boy's grip and went forward, into the ground where it ploughed the grass of the hill, catching on a bump, vaulting the wagon like a catapult.

It would have been worth seeing, that handle sticking into the ground and the wagon vaulting up, throwing the three boys into the blue morning sky, towards the sleeping town, as they separated in the air, falling into a matching trinity of blue jeans and white shirts.

The boys are statues broken on the hill and the wagon is bent and buckled. The wagon is upside down, wheels still turning. The hard shiny black handle has severed, and it lies furthest down the hill, like a dark key. The sky will be spinning around and they are bruised but not cut. They gather back around the wagon. Two of them are crying, the third turns the wagon upright. One retrieves the handle and puts it into the wagon. They try to push the wagon but it has buckled too badly to move. They carry the wagon over to the pinewood and take it deep into the trees, leaving it there.

Then, they walk as one towards the waking town.

The youngest: no I never forgot. I didn't want to do it. Still don't know why we did. Trying to prove something to somebody but nobody knew but us. We cried for our pride, our broken wagon. I've felt the shame. But I'm no stranger to shame. I walked out on everything and am still walking. I deliberately lost touch years ago and sometimes it is just better to leave things the way they are. I think about that wagon a lot, the way we just left it among the trees on the hill and not one of us ever went back to look, to see if it is still there. When adults asked about our new Christmas wagon we said it was stolen from our own backyard one night. My uncle was angry but not at us. He even accused one or two kids, and spoke to their parents. That was just one more thing to be ashamed of. Something began that day and stayed with all of us. I think the wagon would fill with water and that the black handle would lie in the bottom. It would fill with rain and snow. The rain and snow would stay for years. Birds would drink from it, bathe in it: finches, robins, bobolinks, blackbirds. It would begin to rust until the shiny red turned to rust. The handle would do the same. The rust would eat holes through the wagon and the holes would grow larger. The rubber tyres would erode away but this would take years, there in the shelter of the pines. It would fill with pine needles, bird shit. I think its skeleton could still be there but maybe the park janitor would have found it in the first few days and junked it. No, I think it is still there, so much part of the pine plantation that it has reverted to the ground, the soil. "Red Flyer" would have melted from its side, the first to go within a year or two, leaving a livid scar where the letters had been. Just a livid scar, the whole memory of that and everything that came after that…

Concerning the eldest:

He was the only one left alive they said, when our unit arrived. But he was in the jungle and we couldn't find him. I would never go out there alone at night, what with the cobras and tigers. I had a guard dog who used to bark like hell at night and we thought it might be Viet Cong but it was usually a big spitting cobra, once, a tiger. My dog also used to go crazy at those big leeches you saw everywhere. That kid used to run barefoot a lot in the jungle, not wise, but he'd leave them all standing flat-footed. I don't like to think of him being out there alone, I hope he died quickly. Somebody said the Cong might have taken him back to Hanoi as a prisoner but his name never came up again on any list of prisoners of war... We had "R and R"- Rest and Recuperation - together in Singapore. A good meal, a few drinks, a few girls. Nice guy, Canadian originally I think. He once talked about this red wagon he had as a kid. Tried to take it down a mountain or big hill and almost killed himself and his two brothers. An odd thing to talk about on the streets of Singapore so it must have been an important memory to him. I lost touch with him after that. Then we were called in to look for survivors after the firefight. Nobody found alive. I also like to think he would have survived out there on his own, one of the few I know who could. Said he liked to run barefoot because it made his feet never touch the ground, "leaving the pain down on earth where it belonged." He joked that one thing he wanted to do before he died was to go back and see if his little red wagon was where he hid it! I'm heartsick about the whole thing. I might go there one day, for him, look for that red wagon on the hill. He described the thing so well that I think I can almost smell those lodgepole pines in the rain, in the warm Spring earth.

The man on the hillside is conscious again in his own broken red car, its black bits, shining with rain, scattered over the hill. Maybe he is the last of the boys. He only wants to get out of the car and walk somewhere, and keep walking. Walk away from everything, down, downhill.

The Great Bear of Istanbul, and other stories

The bear is brown, ragged, looks like an exploded mattress. There is a rope around his muzzle and neck. A man holds the other end of the short rope. The rope is fluffed out and filthy, like the bear.

The man holding the rope is sitting on a building block. The bear is sitting in the dust. Every so often, the man sets down his teacup then grips the rope half way along its length and uses the folded over length as a whip. He whips the bear, which roars and swipes at him.

The bear roars. The man laughs. The gathered crowd laughs. I see all this from my window. I laugh too. At the whole thing. The man. The crowd. The bear. She speaks after a long pause.

"You should see a doctor. I know dysentery when I see it."

"It's not dysentery, just a mild food bug."

She looks out the window at the bear.

"So that's what you've been laughing at?" She raises an eyebrow. Her raised eyebrow is clearly two inches above the other one. I look away.

"I . . . I wasn't really laughing at the bear. That would be cruel. I was laughing . . . laughing at the situation."

"Well, it's a situation I'm going to stop."

"You can't go out there. It's none of our business."

"Not yours maybe, but mine. I wouldn't expect you to come anyway, what with your mild tummy bug and all." She slams the room door.

I truly believe I only have an upset stomach. She says it is *definitely* dysentery. With her, it always has to be something other than what is. For her, nothing slips by. For me, this is Istanbul. There is a poor man, with a rope around the neck of a bear. That is all there is. I rush to the toilet. Then I go back to the window.

She is out there now. White t-shirt, jeans, sandals. She seems so small in that crowd of men and boys. The minarets tower above them all. The sky, once blue, is now turning oily grey. The man is looking at her, and the bear is sitting in the dust, drinking from the same teacup the man was drinking from. I smile at that. The bear drinking from the man's cup.

They are talking now but she doesn't know any Turkish.

They will be speaking German. Many Turks worked in Germany in the 70's. She points to the bear. The man takes his cloth cap off and swings it towards the bear, like a horse brushing flies away with its tail. I need to go out but I am too dizzy to move. I clutch the window ledge but keep watching. The man bows a little, looking embarrassed. She looks to the crowd, the bear, the man, then turns back towards the room where we are staying.

I already know what she will say. That I have dysentery and should do something about it, before it gets worse. I will reply that there is nothing I can do, that it is probably only a minor touch of food poisoning. It will go away of itself. Then we will talk about the bear, the man and the rope, how she went out and I didn't or couldn't. I will think that her intervention made no difference to the man or the bear. But I will not say that aloud. Not to her.

Outside, the bear is dancing and the men are laughing and clapping. Hearing her footsteps at the door and seeing the door handle turn, my throat hurts, throbs, like someone is tightening a rope around my neck.

Down Pit

A dog. A bus. A drunk. Newsagent. Chip shop. Bingo. A song
filters through.

> *"When I first went into the dirt,*
> *I had not a penny nor an old pit shirt,*
> *Now I've gotten two or three,*
> *The Walker Pit's done right by me . . ."*

Miner's cottages once defined this square and its town. The
cottages are all gone, leaving fag ends and chip wrappers. I keep
the birth certificate in an old hinged whisky box. I take it out
now and then. The father signed his name but his wife could not
read or write. Her **"X"** is uncertain, shaky, fading. Her eight sons
all went down pit but one, the one who went to university to
become a teacher. My great-grandfather.

One whose lungs went black,

One who lost a leg.

One blinded…

The Walker Pit's done nowt for me.

One went East, One went West. *Gone west. Go west young man.*
Fur trapper slang for dying. One of the mining brothers trundled
down the square, pit piece in his bucket, boots scraping sparks
on the cobbles, last seen walking west into Cumberland, then
down to Liverpool then shipping out to San Francisco, with no
place to go after that. He wrote home twice then was never
heard from again. But that was in his lifetime.

In my lifetime, I went to San Francisco and stood in front of
the San Francisco Opera House.

Postcard One.

The air is fragrant in Spring, due to fresh sea breezes and the
aroma of wisteria, lilac and bougainvillea. A man stands firmly
in all this, against the gentle tolerance of a San Francisco spring
evening. He is dressed in a Nazi uniform, covered in swastikas.
Surprised tourists take photos of him. He is guarding a past, his
past. Mentally, he has gone west and can go no further. That's
what happens in this city. People go as far as they can.

Postcard Two.

When it rains, these old men come into the Public Library
reading room, seeking the latest Croatian and Serbian news-

papers. The men hang their thick tweed coats on chairs facing the hissing gold radiators. They mumble in counterpoint to the radiator hiss. They play chess and drink from coffee-splotched thermos flasks. The men rise in cadres of two and three and go out to smoke on the library steps. Further down the steps are the elders, grandchildren and great-grandchildren of the great Salish tribe who netted salmon near where this building stands. They roll empty beer bottles down the steps. The shards of broken bottle glass shine in the rain and sun, looking like the scales of great totemic fishes from a tribal past.

The Northumberland miner probably arrived by train. He found a guesthouse.

"A room for a week, sir?"

"Two dollars will do it."

"Can a man wash and shave?"

"There's a room on your floor for that. You from England?"

"I was—yes, I am. I was a miner."

"No coal here sir but plenty work for an honest Englishman."

A bath. A shave. A new suit of clothes. Not a penny nor an old pit shirt. Not two or three but one clean shirt will do. He thinks. *Clothes maketh the man.* Today he has left his clean room of oak trim, with its view out to the sea and turquoise sky. Already he has seen colours he has never seen before. He laughs at the poor state of the pit boots he wore all the way from Cumbria. He will never need to go down pit again. He bought a new pocket watch and pair of shoes today. He will sleep well. He will find a good job tomorrow.

****

I am on the Bay Area Rapid Transport system, BART, down the escalator into the glistening colours of a child's party. Down the escalator into the colour of money and speed. Down and down.

****

The sepia photographs of the days after the earthquake captured the rising smoke from fissures in the earth. The gas mains caught fire so that the men staring at the cameras look charred and blackened, like men in hell: Irish gombeen men, dazed police and firemen, Chinese silent and knowing. Soon the Bubonic Plague will actually break out in Chinatown but that will be well-hidden in the official health records for the time being. The homeless all line up for soup as the city burns behind them, even as the wealthy people come down to view the carnage that left their own mansions safe.

I reckon my great-grandfather's brother Thomas had a last smoke in bed, grinning at his old pit boots one last time. Then the earth rent; he went down.

Ward Seven

"Ward Six" was Anton Chekhov's (1860-1904) famous story (1892) about the inmates in a Russian insane asylum. His Doctor Ragin, through his refusal to improve conditions there, ends up an inmate himself. He dies after being beaten by the cruel caretaker Nikita. Without resorting to caricature, Chekhov's disturbing story served as a riposte to Tolstoy's doctrine of non-resistance to evil. It is said Chekhov changed his own opinions after visiting the penal colonies of Sakhalin Island and witnessing first-hand the wretched conditions there.

I was in Ward Seven but you've probably only heard of Ward Six. Chekhov wrote about it. He told us how old Nikita beat Dr. Ragin to death. Ragin believed that evil should not be resisted so perhaps such a violent death was his natural fate. If Ragin had come to our ward he might have been spared because Nikita didn't hold sway here like he did in Ward Six. I agree with Anton Chekhov though. Sometimes, we simply have to fight evil — resist it or die.

Although Doctor Ragin loved good conversation, all of us in Ward Seven had either lost our power of speech or had never had it in the first place. Otherwise, we had everything else that Ward Six had: bedbugs, lice and cockroaches. It smelled exactly the same: mould, urine, sour cabbage and ammonia. Our beds were also screwed to the floor. We were branded *lunatics.* When Nikita was not bullying us, we were simply ignored. We were the silent ones. The hopeless ones. *Beyond redemption* we were told.

Breakfast: a mug of tea.

Lunch: sour cabbage soup and porridge.

Supper: cold slabs of porridge left over from lunch.

Sometimes, a barber came.

I'll introduce the inmates since you would wait forever for anyone else to do it. One was Strekoza, The Dragonfly. He had big bulging eyes, was cadaverous, balding, in his forties. He hovered, looked startled, and then was gone. He did everything quickly but always seemed to be waiting for something dramatic. He had been a fur trapper in the Taiga, having trapped bears, wolves and tigers. He was brought here starving, speechless and naked. He had been here the longest. We never attempted to halt the Dragonfly or to impede him in any way. Old Nikita tried to grab him once but The Dragonfly cast him aside like a fly. The Dragonfly was a true force of nature.

The second was a heavy man, The Whistler, a Tartar I think, who sat cross-legged like a holy man on the floor, rocking to and fro, whistling and making high-pitched noises. He ate greedily, like a pig, slurping and spilling. Nikita beat him regularly but this only elicited high-pitched squeals from the inmate. The Whistler stayed in his own world and was the most harmless of all of us. That's why Nikita beat him.

Third was The Arranger. A tall, gaunt youth who spent all of his day precisely arranging things. He even arranged dead cockroaches carefully for burial. Arranger ate his porridge cautiously, scraping the bowl, setting his spoon down in an exact way. If Arranger's arrangements were thwarted, ten men could not hold him down until the thing was made right, until his arrangement was restored. Nikita let Arranger do various cleaning chores, stacking old mattresses, removing vermin, tidying furniture. Arranger would work all day at one small task, study it, frown, and then begin it all over again.

Fourth was Archangel, an ancient Old Believer from the Caucasus, who came closest to speech of all of us, speaking in a "language" of his own making, mumbling to an angel who apparently never left his side. When Archangel first came here, he insisted on food for his angel but when that was refused, gave his own food to his celestial friend, preferring to go without. Fearing the old man would starve, doctors insisted that his wish be indulged. Once the food was presented, the old man would eat his own but lose interest in the angel's food entirely. The food was removed, to be eaten for the next meal. You'd think angels would prefer something other than sour cabbage or porridge?

Me? Mikhail. Aged 30, the only child of a civil servant and a mother who was born into serfdom. My father worked in a big office where he copied documents. He was a tidy writer but my mother never learned to read or write. How proud they were when I went to St. Petersburg as a medical student but how shamed they were when I joined the *Narodnaya Volya* ("The People's Will") and was convicted of plotting to assassinate Czar Alexander II. Barely twenty, I was sentenced to be executed by firing squad.

The firing squad marched three of us to the edge of a forest.

My two companions were already blindfolded. My blindfold was to be put in place for my execution but clearly my executioners wanted me to see the others die first. It was one of those early spring days in Russia, everything the colour of cold rain. The slender birches. I thought of the line from the old Russian folk song "The Birch is my Mother." I heard a lark singing. His song filled the dull day. A river sparkled in the distance.

The first, Stephan, stepped forward, defiant, shouting "Narodnaya Vol…" Shots crackled and echoed across the forest. He fell to his knees, blood-spattered, dead. He looked so small then, against the river and sky.

Petya was next. I could see him shaking in the cold. He had a wry smile on his childlike face, barely visible under his fine child's hair blowing across it. Of all of us, I felt Petya did not need to be here, that somehow he should have found a different way. He was too gentle to be an assassin or terrorist. When he was shot one of the bullets tore out of him, turning him sideways. I saw clearly his little boy's face which a razor would now never touch. He was still shivering, shaking like a tiny bird with a broken wing.

The forest lark was quiet for a brief time after the shot, but then began singing again. I don't remember much else. My nose was itching and I wanted to scratch it. They put the blindfold on. It was itchy around my ears. The man putting it on joked with me. "Your head is too bloody big for the blindfold. Your big head. That's what got you into this mess in the first place."

I smiled at the joke and at the thought of a man wanting still to scratch his nose seconds before his eternal death. I heard the shots. I slumped to my knees. Silence. Then the same small bird began singing as it had after Petya's execution. Mine had been staged to be only a *mock execution*, to "teach me a lesson."

I heard later my father knew someone higher up in the Civil Service who managed to intervene on my behalf and persuade the authorities of my feckless nature. It had been a student prank he said. This boy is mentally unstable he argued. After the execution, my hair had turned white and I could no longer speak. I had trouble eating and sleeping. I was hearing voices. Instead of going to work in Siberia as was expected, I was brought to Ward Seven.

The first night, Nikita had attempted to kick me in the ribs. "You would murder our Czar, ordained of God, you nihilist scum." I grabbed his leg and overturned him then moved as if to step on his head. He left me alone after that, as beaten bullies do. I pretended to be worse than I was. I sometimes even ate live cockroaches to create an air of menace about myself. I deliberately rolled my head from side to side, tongue sticking out. I soon adapted to life in the ward, which has been better than the life I had as a student. It gave my mother one less mouth to feed and at last, here I was "of the people." I knew I could not live this way forever. I also hoped and knew that my speech would return one day and that I might find a way to be free. Doctor Ragin could have understood somehow but all the same he never came often into our ward. He never suggested major improvements. He allowed us to continue to live in filth and be bitten by vermin. He must have known Nikita beat some of the patients but the doctor never tried to stop it. I could have written all this down for him. I could have used sign language. I would have convinced him of the necessity for fighting, for resistance. Our task is to identify what evil we will choose to resist and how best to do it. Because choosing is not always easy doesn't mean we should do nothing but Doctor Ragin chose to do nothing.

When I stood on the forest edge expecting my life to be over at the age of twenty the voice of that tiny bird rejoicing at the end of winter made me think I had not really resisted evil. I had merely tried to kill the very Czar who had freed the serfs and had given Russia more democracy than it had ever had. But allowing a drunken Nikita to rob from you and beat you and mistreat you is simply cowardice, *not* non-resistance to evil. It is not as noble as turning the other cheek. Even Count Tolstoy would have resisted such treatment.

Sometimes, just one angry look from me saved The Whistler from a beating. Just one look from me made Nikita leave The Dragonfly alone in peace. That is when I vowed that I would destroy Nikita. Not for revenge for Doctor Ragin but as part of my escape plan. I then devoted every waking moment to how I could do this without giving up my own life or freedom. I will now tell you how Doctor Ragin, Chekhov's misguided man, accidentally made this possible.

In Ward Six one day Dr. Ragin had summoned Nikita to him. "In Ward Seven, Nikita, there is the former student Mikhail who should take regular exercise to help restore his mental health. I want you to obtain a ball and take him out, in all weathers, to play ball. A half hour each day should do it. Fresh air and exercise will be enough to cure him."

Although Nikita always slavishly followed orders, he grumbled and threatened me. "My little assassin, you can't hide behind the good doctor forever. I will play ball with you for now but the time will come when I shall shove the ball down your throat or strangle you with it. *Voice of the People* my arse. I *am* one of "The People" but you don't speak for me." I knew then it would have to be me or Nikita, that I would suffer the same fate as Dr.Ragin if Nikita caught me off guard.

But we played ball. Nikita would kick the ball to me and I would kick it back or he would throw it to me and I would throw it back. It was then I noticed something I could use against Nikita in the future. Sometimes he would deliberately kick the ball far enough for me to turn my back to him and begin the long run to retrieve it. I would steal a glimpse of Nikita secretly reaching into his shabby military coat, swigging from a small bottle. *Vodka*. It was to prove Nikita's downfall and my salvation. Something else happened during this time which made me even more determined to see my "project" through.

I had forbidden my elderly mother to visit me for the distress it would cause her. Meanwhile, my father had coped with my incarceration in a very different way. One day, at his desk, after his usual lunch of black bread and cheese, my father cut his wrists and bled to death. He used enough blotting paper to prevent a mess and actually left a few kopecks as payment for the blotting paper he had taken from the company stores. This unspectacular man had plead for my life and then taken his own.

After my father's death, Nikita would catch my attention and make a cutting motion across his wrists. His smirk made me strengthen my resolve to both kill him and obtain my freedom at the same time.

Over the next years my "friends" on the outside had offered to help me escape but gradually, they were all arrested, transported or executed. But I also had enough links to the outside world to obtain and hide small bottles of vodka. This was "country" vodka, the kind I had grown up with, made in stills and cylinders which often contained a lot of lead and other poisonous metals. The peasants who drank this stuff gradually went blind or deaf, or became insane due to the slow attrition of lead poisoning. It was this noxious vodka I offered Nikita each time we played football. He drank it prodigiously, unaware of its foul taste or content. I had him now. From the moment he first accepted drink from me, he and I were in collusion. He could now neither beat nor threaten me. It took a long time but medical student that I was, I saw the sure early signs of lead poisoning: slurred speech, forgetfulness, volatile temper. Meanwhile old Nikita's downward spiral had good results for me. My brain grew less troubled and in the quiet of the ward at night, I found I could speak to myself. My own speech was returning. I spoke the names of the inmates first. *Dragonfly, The Arranger, The Whistler.* I spoke Doctor Ragin's name, and Chekhov's.

I was ready for my next move. I had requested a visit from Father Grigory in order to make confession. The old priest duly came, looking impatient with the place and proceedings. He knew a bit about my past. He looked sceptical that I could speak a proper confession to him. I kneeled before the old man. I began slowly, in a weak and croaking voice. Gradually, my words gained strength and clarity.

"Oh Father, I have sinned against the Regal Family of Russia, against God and the Russian people. I have shamed my mother. I have caused my own father's death. Through prayer, I have come to contrition before God. In return, He has given me my speech and reason back. You can now hear the miracle for yourself. After ten years, my speech has been given back to me in order to confess my sins. God bless the Czar and his family. God bless Mother Russia. God bless this asylum!"

Grigory reeled back as if shocked. "This violent lunatic, this criminal is the product of divine intervention! He is indeed proof of a miracle! From being a criminal assassin, he has turned to God! He shall not be turned away!"

I smiled to myself. My confession, although not entirely sincere, had worked. But I had meant most of it, especially that to do with my own parents.

Immediately the wealthy local church gave money to the asylum. Not to be outdone, the wealthy landowners followed suit. The old mattresses and furniture were burned. The ward was painted. A new diet was introduced. The wards were rid of cockroaches and vermin. Beatings were forbidden. Old Nikita's role was reduced to that of a janitor, cleaning the floors and emptying the slop buckets. Doctors began to see the patients again and recommend a new regime for each.

In Ward Six, Doctor Ragin had allowed himself to be defeated by the institution and by his fellow doctors. He was thus finally beaten to death by the wretched Nikita. Now Nikita's brain had wasted so much that he himself was given a bed in the ward, where he smoked his pipe and snarled. His hands had begun to shake badly.

Through Grigory's influence, my ultimate pardon was obtained, after ten years, two months and twenty-three days in Ward Seven. What a difference my resistance had made. The ward glistened. The Arranger and The Dragonfly seemed more purposeful. The Whistler's face had acquired a sublimity and peace. In their own sad ways, the inmates even tried to communicate with one another, with sign language and body movements.

My last night there I barely slept. I dreamt of a forest full of wild, free-running deer. I awoke, refreshed and clear-headed. I crept over to Nikita's bed. I strangled him to death.

It was later assumed he had drunk himself to death since there were no witnesses. In truth nobody now cared about Nikita's fate. They buried him a few days after I left, in a grave not far from Doctor Ragin's. Only the gravedigger was present at his funeral.

Inter-City Blues:
Eight Gone Postcards

PARIS. The men and women are dark. It is Spring. They laugh with eyes and teeth wrapped in light blue light. They dance something like a samba around a man who is lying in the gutter. None of us can know if the man in the gutter is alive or dead; but the men and women *are alive* and singing. The woman's high heel leaves a hard white triangle on the gutter man's left hand but still he does not move.

SAN FRANCISCO. The entire city is wallpapered in pastel — blue, green, pink and peach. The city is coloured in ripe fruit. The sky is ridiculous in a blue that does not exist anywhere else; blue with a tight white cap. The sea is bulging with fat fish. At noon, one man is standing against a dark stone building. The man is covered in swastikas. His eyes are blue but not the same blue as the sky and sea. In all of the city, there is no brown to match his shirt. A gentle pink giraffe could sniff at the man and wonder what he is doing here for he is not a happy man. If tourists took snapshots, they would tell the giraffe to move so they could photograph clearly this strange man in brown, red and black.

ISTANBUL. There is a man with a dancing bear which will not dance despite a man prodding it with a sharp stick. The bear is watching two boys punch and gouge each other while shining a tourist's shoes. One boy shines the left shoe, the other, the right shoe. Each wants to shine both shoes. Old men watch the bear, while loosening their grip on the leather slings which hold cargoes of new dishwashers bound for grand hotels on the European side. Around this are moving 1953 Studebakers with all seats removed, to make way for cargoes of dates and plums and men with fine teeth done by dentists years before in Bonn. The men crouching in the Studebaker remember living 15 to a room in Cologne, and watching young German women doing stripteases. Finally, the bear dances.

DUBLIN. November night. A layer of rain on the street, a layer of light on the rain. A man has not eaten for three days but he will eat tonight. His fingers — tines of a muddied fork — grip the

74

Brussels sprouts in his pocket. The sprouts roll gently against his thigh. He will return to a battered caravan and eat them. He is descended from the great royal poet, Feidhlimidh, son of Dall, story teller to Conchobhar. The man will not get back to the caravan in time to meet a Japanese Zen Buddhist student who is sheltering there from the cold rain. The student is boiling rice over a primus stove. He will leave some of the rice for whoever lives there. He will leave a heron made of folded blue paper atop the bowl of rice. The man stumbles on the shining light; he munches a raw sprout. Its juice feeds his royal blood.

MONTREAL. There is a black wrought-iron railing around a balcony. The balcony is at a second floor window. It is noon on a busy road. There is a drive-in burger restaurant to the right of the house which has the balcony. Beefy men in red lumberjack shirts phone in their orders, in English. The balcony looks like New Orleans or Paris. There is a woman in the window. She is shouting in French to the sky. She is naked from the waist up and is shaking a sheet out the window. No, she is not shouting but singing. The dust from the sheet settles onto the roofs of the cars of the men phoning in their orders.

BONN. A gaggle of men in cheap blue suits huddle in front of the SEX KINO, which will open soon. The young men grin with fine teeth, visible against the blue cloth. Inside, in the dark, they wonder at the tall women on the screen, so different from their wives and sisters. The older men remain outside, on benches by the river. They speak Kermanji. Each has a private motion picture inside his own head; each has a cinema of bright poppies, turquoise and snow leopards. Further along the Rhine, a blind man plays Beethoven on a huge crosscut saw. The older Kurdish men listen. They know Beethoven was born here but his soul, they say, was Kurdish — definitely Kurdish.

TEHERAN. The alley is next to a market where people buy fruit and spices which they carry in bags made of straw. The bags swing in strange arcs, in strange gyrations — because the men, women and children swinging them are missing fingers, hands and feet. One says: "Ask the police and the Golden Peacock Throne for our fingers and hands back; then our bags will behave themselves." Some of the fruit is melting in the sun. Its juice is dripping onto the stone pavement. Scorpions scuttle forth to drink the juice, risking the crippled rhythms above them.

THESSALONIKA. A woman dressed in black gave me figs. She rode a donkey. A great tortoise crossed the dusty road. Along that road, fires rise higher than the dust. The campfires of gypsies from Bulgaria. The curve of their camp is higher than the clean whit a woman with a skirt of blue and blouse of white. She dazzles the gypsy eyes, she sparkles. She blinds them. In the heat, they will begin to remove their clothes. She is cool; sea breezes kiss her under her clothes; she is refreshed.

Raindust Two

Bo Cooley was saying this as he carved an adder from a piece of Lochaber oak.

"See that rain falling? Every raindrop raising one particle of dust is really one soul going out of this world. If we try, we can remember a few tiny dust motes rising – but only a few. It is forgetting that we humans do best."

Bo talked liked that all the time. We were used to it. The wood curved away from his knife like potato peelings.

"But I remember every funeral I went to. Aunt Grace, Jamie. I remember them all."

"Oh aye. Them close to us and maybe a few famous ones too. Kennedy, John Lennon. But of the millions of raindrops falling and souls leaving we do not remember many. That is for our own good."

Bo was right as usual. I sat down and could only come up with two names.

Mao

Mao was dead, inside a newspaper kiosk in Thessalonica, under a sky more blue than the lips of a dead man. The Greek letters said *Mao is Dead*. I bought a paper for a few drachmas and spread it out on the hot promenade pavement. The sea was calm. Seagulls swooped above my head. One shit near Mao's head. I thought Mao looked a bit like Sitting Bull. Mao, a farmer's son, just like me. Greek sailors sauntered past. Men sold roasted chestnuts, balloons, or tiny squares of baklava. Greek women in billowing skirts of green, red and yellow walked arm in arm. I bought a slice of baklava. Meanwhile, Mao rose slowly from the page. I helped him up, gave him my arm. I gave him a bite of my baklava, and then let him totter away like an infant on new legs, away into the sailors, the girls and the blue Greek morning.

Elvis

Southern Indiana, August 1977. In a clearing ringed with sassafras, poplar, hickory and maple, there is a picnic table groaning with food. The cicadas have not yet begun their great boiling chorus. Fireflies sleep deep in the forest, before they flicker like dying stars. On the table: fried chicken, potato salad, great stacks of corn on the cob, milk gravy, deep-fried catfish, hushpuppies, chittlins, rice and more. There are great sweating jugs of iced tea with floating lemon. But nobody is eating or drinking. A large woman is sobbing. "Elvis is Dead. The King is Dead." The food remains untouched while great swallowtail butterflies hover over the table. Catbirds streak through hickory trees. "Elvis is Dead," sob people, while all around life is clicking, chirping, sucking nectar. Elvis would understand this. He would know what to say to the big inconsolable woman. He would be happy among the food and like a truly great king, he would cry with his people.

Bo Cooley, I remembered twice but who now remembers the living oak branch before it became a serpent in your hands?

Rory Angel

"I'm a million miles away . . ." Rory Gallagher

I climbed out of the hotel window into the German night. **Come back, come back, Neevie,** they both shouted but I was well up the footpath and into the vineyards by then. I threw my dress and tights into the dark Rhine and took jeans and boots from my rucksack, which I had managed to grab on the way out the window. I shivered all night, listening to small trains go up the valley. Church bells rang, Rhine barges growled, splashing big waves onto the shore.

* * * *

The great heat of 1976, Europe gripped in drought, water rationed, and vine leaves curling like tobacco. The next day I walked and walked until I began to hear German again in my head, natural to me with a German mother and Irish truck-driving father. They would miss me for a while but would not bother to go to the police, who would of course wonder how my mother got such swollen black eyes and a broken jaw. Each day was the same. I walked past tourists in their slacks and floral dresses, eating their ice cream while I kept my eyes downwards, just in front of my hiking boots. I slept rough in my sleeping bag, eaten by insects in forests of pine and chestnut. The river barges and valley trains kept me awake but often lulled me to sleep too. I had just enough money for fruit, chocolate and tobacco which I also easily nicked from kiosks and outdoor stands.

(And where was it – when was it, when the old man was kinder and didn't yet hit my mother? I was sitting high in the lorry cab, my legs not touching the cab floor, listening to the old eight-track tapes. "Rory Gallagher, a Donegal Man just like myself," said my da proudly: This I can remember from the tape)

Livin' like a trucker, for a month or more.
Queuein' at the diner, never find a seat
Singin' for my supper, but I never get to eat
Closin' all the windows, keepin' out the rain.

* * * *

No rain at all, that summer, grass wilting, flowers drooping, river turning green and slimy. I was frightened of the German police—*Die Bullen*—so I kept myself hidden during the nights.

I began to stink and itch, then my period came. I was ill, shivering in a chestnut forest, high above the Rhine. My teeth clattered in my head. I stank of sweat and blood. I rose to lean against a tree. Dizzy, I went from tree to tree, down to the shore. Birds rustled. Town bells rang the time. I heard an owl. A small night train vanished around the mountain. A barge charged through the fog. I was naked in the heat, the way I always slept. My hair was like steel wool. I felt my sharp ribs and small breasts. I walked into the river, until it was no longer warm from the sun but cold, the current faster. I threw myself forward, kneeling, sinking into deep water. I think I was there a long time. I saw trains come and go, and heard bells until they rang no more. Barges sent waves to me and I walked into the sweetness of the cold water, backwards into the warm water, washing all the filth and smell away, washing my blood from me, and shaking my hair like a puppy. I knelt down, face into the cold water. I saw the moon floating on the river. Then sleep came with a last bell and a last train vanishing into the night above the sleeping village.

At dawn, I was choking in water, struggling to crawl onto the slippery shore. I had no strength and felt the river pulling me back. Then I saw *him* grinning down at me. Him, a boy in a red flannel shirt, a face round and cheerful. Rory Gallagher, That is, *a poster* of Rory Gallagher. He was everywhere that summer of 1976, his poster on every wall, lamp post, building scaffold and tree. And so that was that, live or dead, not caring, I was reborn, crawling naked onto a beach in Germany, and my deliverer, saviour, midwife — guardian ANGEL— was Rory Gallagher, on a poster where no poster should have been. I washed my clothes and hung them over a chestnut branch to dry. I felt clean and new.

There were still a few bad nights after that one. Once, I awoke near Cochem to see an old tramp wanking over my sleeping bag, while I was in the bushes taking a pee.

A hotel owner near St. Goarhausen threw a bucket of mop water over me, calling me a tramp and a whore.

Then, one day, I was eating a plum when I heard a voice in German saying "I quit."

Another voice pleaded: "But you can't just go."

The girl who said *I quit* pointed at me saying *she'll do.*

And *I did.* Became a waitress at Gino's, in tights and a sky blue dress, me serving good Italian ice cream and coffee, given fat tips from fatter tourists, and Gino in bed with his young wife with the window open so all their loving sounds could float over the pavement cafe below.

I had phoned home by this time. Mum had a job and had left dad, who had quit drinking and was taking counseling treatment for his violence and temper.

"He is changing but I am happier now on my own. I miss you, Neevie."

Days off, into the cities and there would be Rory, grinning down from the walls and lamp posts: in Bonn, Cologne, Koblenz, and it was a pact, between the two of us, that all my spare change went to beggars, who in that summer, were everywhere.

I left Gino's in September when all the leaves were changing and the fields and vineyards were becoming a different colour. I a walked up to a vineyard shrine and put some flowers there, below a parched, thirsty Jesus — then finally went home to Ireland.

* * * *

I studied to become a psychiatric nurse and often looked down, smiling on patients, sometimes pulling them up from drowning in their own deep rivers the way Rory pulled me up all those years ago.

One day, I heard they wheeled Rory into surgery and that final time, he could not be saved the way he saved me. At 47, with a lot of joy and music left in him, he was dead.

But there is another way of seeing, another way of looking at all this. Housewives in the soft rain of Cork scurried past you, Rory. Dark Moluccans in Rotterdam sheltered under your poster; Kurds in Bonn took you as a brother, Turks in Cologne drank their tea in your company and this small girl along the Rhine saw life in your face, and took it. Always, the poster was TONIGHT or TOMORROW or NEXT WEEK, always the FUTURE.

And each poster peeled, only to be covered up by another poster, another singer, another circus, another guitarist. By then, time would no longer matter — past, present or future — because your poster would always be somewhere in the world, and would rise to the top again, after the wind, rain and sun had done their work. Somewhere, from Cork to Amsterdam, to the far Danube, you are slowly rising to the surface; a million miles away now, but alive as any angel.

Pecan Macintyre

"Bigger than a coffin, not as wide as a church door." Who said that? Marcuse? He must have been talking about my box room—my home—my world—for most of my life so far. I am now closing three doors to that life.

Door One. Box room door, opens to the kitchen.

Door Two. Kitchen door, opens to the hall.

Door Three. Opens from the hall to the landing. Our "front" door.

Flat 3 (TCF). Top floor, centre flat, or, third floor, centre flat.

Key locks the door of hard dark varnish, peeling like black sunburnt skin around the tarnished brass nameplate—our name—MACINTYRE. I leave it for the new owners. Who knows? Maybe they will be "MacIntyre" as well. I drop the key through the letterbox.

One last look. The landing. TLF. The family "LISTER," here before me, still here. But no nameplate on TRF—a succession of students, flat mates and lodgers.

Then, down the stairs; door bells, iron rails, peeling green pastel walls against the dark stone of scrubbed stairs and floor, scrubbed to a white grain, like a salt-sand beach, and down to the bright green blistered door, which opens to the street, never locked in all my days there, long final dark hall leading to it also scrubbed—the smell of Dettox only slightly stronger than the smell of drunkard piss, dog fur and exhaust fumes coming in from the street.

I am on the street, suitcase in hand; like so many of my people before me; taxi, Waverley Station, bus, airport.

Cabbie. Ginger like me. A bit older. I'm 32.

-America, eh?-

I have a job there.

Lucky bugger. Nae life here.

(I don't tell him I may not stay there. I work in Disease Control—plenty of diseases to keep me busy—but I may not stay. Not for me, Disney World, the Grand Canyon, Florida. I will go to the deep red clay of Georgia, find a pecan tree and stroke its rough brown bark and downy leaves; then, I will either remember, forget or understand—and any of those things will be good.

****

Thomas J. MacIntyre, my old man, now dead from the fags; he got greyer and smaller every year and coughed and died. Wee squat dark man—he always said he was the last of the Picts—a good man, hard worker, the eternal punter. Forklift driver and mechanic. From Inverness, a long time ago (for his sins, a Caley supporter) and I can still hear his Inverness speech "the purest English spoken," he would laugh and I remember when computers were becoming popular hearing him first say the word "computer." Pure English? "Campewerr." Maybe. I miss him.

Mother, Rona, bonny and red, grew up in the same flat in the same room as me, died two months ago to the day. She was the flat, the cladding, mortar and dark wood of the place and I could never believe it would survive her, that I would one day drop the key through a letter box for another owner; the final soft thud of it, from myself, Kevin "Box Room" MacIntyre.

My father was from a big family. His brother James, my uncle—merchant navy, wanderer, supposed flawed genius, married a woman in Savannah, Georgia then unsuccessfully farmed peaches and peanuts before settling on pecan nuts, becoming, we'd heard, "The Pecan King of Georgia."

And one Spring day, James MacIntyre, ex-merchant seaman and Pecan King crossed our polished brass threshold, bringing a rust-red cloth bag of shelled pecan nuts for us. His daughter Catherine was with him. She was five years older than me. I was six.

James was tall, thin and dark—entirely unlike my father. After greetings and inquiries the adults went through the door on the right into the living room and Catherine and myself went left into the kitchen and sat down at the table, facing each other from the table ends.

Catherine, thin and dark in a light blue dress, curly black hair and eyes like a cow's—liquid and the perfect brown for her brown skin. A face as open as a deep pool, though at age six, I only remember staring at her.

"I'm Catherine. But nobody calls me that. Everybody calls me Pecan—they say I'm like a pecan pie—hard, dark but sweet. You're my first cousin, Kevin."

Aye.

My dad says that all the time.

Eh?

Says that all the time too.

Pecan?

Not Puh can, but PEE con.

She would see a short, (too white) freckled boy, hair the colour of old copper water pipes; a little scabby boy of no interest to her, my legs not even reaching from the seat to the floor. Our kitchen would interest her more. The tallest and largest room in the flat, all white, natural tiles of beige; heavy drop-leaf table ("early Depression" my mother called it) in one small corner nearest my box room bedroom; a long wall with sink and cabinets. Opposite was the cream-coloured Rayburn, above it the pulley to dry the clothes. At the far wall was a window going from the floor to the tall ceiling, where every visitor would stand at some time, viewing the dark slates and chimney pots of Edinburgh to the far horizon, ending in the bulk of Arthur's Seat.

And Pecan was there. Her curly head haloed by the purple light of Edinburgh in the Spring, a still brown life against the glistening roofs; against the hard slow smoke of the city, making the old volcano seem alive with the illusion of smoke coming from it and not from the city below.

"Y'all got a real mountain in yo kitchen window—a real live mountain."

Her back to me, the curves of her in the soft dress, visible in the window light, in the centre of the slow drifting smoke. . .

We heard the adults laughing in the other room and on that day, Pecan MacIntyre took my sweating freckled hand in her long exquisite fingers—out into the Spring evening of Edinburgh. Turn right, cross one street, past the fruit and vegetable stalls, to the newsagent for sweets. She let go of my hand then, leaving a pale ring around my knuckles.

She took my hand again on the street. I heard a window open across the street, at Iain Doig's house.

"Look at Kevin MacIntyre, holding hands with a nigger."

I felt Pecan's long fingers tighten, tense against my sweating skin. She let go of my hand only when we got back to the flat. I sat crunching sweets while Pecan took her place at the window again.

"Pecan, what's a nigger?"

Her dark eyes burned through my freckles. I never asked her that question again.

I learned later Uncle James had married a black woman from Macon, Georgia. Pecan looked just like her mother.

****

We fed the pecan nuts to the hesitant squirrels in the Royal Botanic Gardens and put the rest out for the hungry birds of Winter, but the red bag of nuts never seemed to diminish much. I did some growing in the meantime, freckles now confused by acne, my room shrinking like a gold fish bowl as I grew. My box room opened to the kitchen in the wall opposite its large window so that my door, fully open, gave me that window view; no other views were possible from my box room: one bed along one wall of the rectangle, chest of drawers against the short wall; small wardrobe and shelves along the wall separating my room from the kitchen. Beyond my chest of drawers must have been the bedroom of the adjoining flat for I could often hear Mr and Mrs Lister on their bed, springs creaking. I heard the rising and falling of grunting and sighing, reminding me of a kitchen kettle shaking as it reaches boiling point, then fading to a satisfied hiss.

****

Uncle James came a few more times, on his own. He was exporting pecan nuts to Britain now. He always left us a grainy red cloth bag of pecans, which vanished slowly into the tight paws of the grey squirrels of the Botanic.

****

I was thirteen and Pecan was 18 when they next came.

Pecan's mother came with them that time. Aunt Sally. Long tall Sally. She had on a light blue summer dress. Her hair was plaited down her back. She was black and striking. I was thirteen, now taller than both my parents. Pecan was now only slightly taller than me. She was dressed in a red flared skirt and white blouse.

(Some things never change in Scotland. Children to the kitchen, adults to the living room). Pecan stood tall against the window.

"Well, Kevin, do you remember the last time you saw me?"

"I do. We went out for sweets."

She laughed and walked over to her flight bag by the table.

"My dad says you're into football and music. Don't know much about football but thought you might like some Georgia music."

It was a treasure she emptied onto the hard scratched wood of the kitchen table. Albums of Little Richard and James Brown.

I mumbled a thanks, still in awe of my dark cousin, who was back at the window.

"Kevin, see all the chimneys, all that smoke. People laughing, crying, loving out there. Standing here, we only see the smoke. Lingers, then blows away. Like us. Through all that you got a mountain in the distance. Some folks have to look hard through all that smoke and rain to see that mountain there. . ."

Then her voice lowered.

"All those dreams out there, over the roof."

Pecan, tall and lean against the window, the rainbow prism of a small tear on her left brown cheekbone.

The door opened, the moment gone. It was Aunt Sally.

"Kevin, I'm gonna show yo momma what to do with pecans. Imagine feedin pecans to squirrels—that's good human food we talkin about—soul food."

My mother hovered giggling, small and red against the window. Pecan and I sat at the kitchen table while our mothers worked on the counter top, mixing and laughing in the dark shadow of Arthur's Seat with:

Butter, brown sugar, three eggs (well-beaten) corn syrup? no? treacle will do, salt, chopped pecan nuts, vanilla. Bake very hot, cool down, serve with cream.

The taste was warm, soft, sugary, yet hard and dark, crunchy, perfect with hot tea; all adults eating quietly, happily at the kitchen table against the dark angry purple of the old volcano and: an awkward goodbye kiss from me on Pecan, my nose glancing off her cheek where lingered a smell something like sugar and pecan, a cheek the colour of milky tea, me still beaming bright red long after the dark door was closed.

****

Pecan came one last time.

I was seventeen, preparing for exams, preparing for University that autumn. It was April and my parents had gone to Inverness for the weekend. I was at the kitchen table. Doorbell, Pecan at the door. As tall as last time, in faded flared jeans, short sleeve light blue blouse, hair in magnificent Afro, bordered by a bright red and black patterned headband. We hugged, went into the kitchen for tea.

Pecan said she had been in London, preparing to go to Biafra as part of a food and medical relief team, hoping to get through the invading Nigerian troops. She'd come up to Edinburgh on her free weekend.

"Kevin, the Biafrans are a nation of poets and musicians— dreamers and thinkers—and the Nigerian government wants to

86

starve the entire nation to death, with British and American help of course. I'm going with a relief team to try get supplies through. It's unofficial and dangerous — in the middle of a war."

I told her of my plans to be a doctor.

"Good man, cousin. I like it. A doctor who can jive to James Brown!"

She placed the very first Allman Brothers record on the table — still impossible to get in Edinburgh.

She stood at the window. Edinburgh Spring afternoon — sun, rain and sky all birled together and we drank wine, made a pecan pie, studied for my exam and played James Brown records.

"Ain't no drag — Kevin's got a brand new bag.... Hey, momma, hey, hey...."

The wine went to my head — I wasn't used to it — and remember waking, fully clothed, in my box room bed. Pecan must have put me there, then gone off to sleep in the living room or other bedroom.

About dawn, I woke, needing the loo. My door was slightly ajar. I could see the early light coming through the kitchen window. Pecan was there. She was dressed in a long white nightgown, her arms to the window, her back to me. I could see her strong dark body through the light cotton. She looked like an angel or a moth, flattened against the glass, crucified. I could hear her crying softly.

I know I was not meant to see or hear her. I did nothing though I wanted to comfort her in some way. I pretended I did not see and quietly turned away from the half-open door. I fell asleep. She was gone when I awoke.

****

I never saw Pecan MacIntyre again. She was last seen alive by the British Red Cross on a dusty famine road. She was on foot, heading for the interior of a country whose people were becoming the smoke of a twilight dream, dispersed forever in the flame of war.

Smoke, blown across the rooftops of the world.

Fascism (with ketchup)

Forgiving evil is the only sin. Granda Gallagher (1888-1970)

Francisco Franco couldn't come to our party although he was clearly invited by Anne-Marie. I heard her say on the phone: "Tell him from me to get his arse out of bed and over here. We're just up from the Hurley Ground, on St. Mary's Street, Galway, County Galway, Ireland, like...."

There wasn't much to eat at the party. We had a few loaves of white bread and this giant black pudding I brought over from Scotland made by Mac . . . Scotland's World Champion Haggis and Black Pudding Maker (the one by the level crossing.)

Who *was* there, even if Franco wasn't? Students from the college (who had just been to a Bothy Band concert) some Bretons, Walshie (wearing a Roman helmet and tunic and holding a plastic sword) Joe "Spanners," Mickey Flamingo, Anne-Marie and an old woman from County Clare who couldn't leave out the letter "n" in words having the letter "u" before the letter "t." A lot of people in Clare do this it seems but the students kept plying her with stout just to keep her talking.

Anne-Marie was furious Franco couldn't leave his deathbed to be with us.

"He *owes* it to Granda," she kept hissing.

Whose Granda?

"**My** granda" she replied.

"He went to Glasgow as a labourer and later joined The International Brigade saying how Hitler, Mussolini and Franco were a disgrace to humanity. Granda swore he'd personally rip Hitler's remaining testicle off. Anyway, they gave Granda a cigarette lighter (inscribed in Govan) with the words:
THIS MACHINE KILLS FASCISTS
The same as the words on Woody Guthrie's guitar, mind."

She is wonderful whispered Joe Spanners, nudging my ribs. Anne-Marie *was* wonderful with her black curls piled up like caviar on her forehead, eyes green but flecked with other green and blue bits, like my prize marbles – *and* she was my cousin after all.

And then it became a black pudding gala event where a party just incidentally broke out. At the kitchen hatch, someone was slipping toast out, drenched in butter and spread with hot fried black pudding topped with ketchup. There was plenty stout and beer to wash it down and the hot toast and black pudding made everyone shiny with sweat. Everyone was grinning or laughing. At one stage, there was just the earnest crunching of toast.

The Breton couple stood on a sturdy table. She put a heel through my toast while he pretended to be a flamenco dancer (with toast in mouth instead of a rose) and they clapped and stamped:

FRAN CO IS DEAD

CLAP ...CLAP..CLAP... CLAP

And everybody was soon clapping it out.

Someone explained. *We heard it on the TV upstairs. Franco just died.*

Joseph Spanners then said a bold thing.

"Man—taste that black pudding. Scotland's finest—and old Franco dying without so much as tasting such a thing, or seeing Anne-Marie, here and now. But why is she so keen on a dead Fascist?"

The Bretons stopped dancing. The clapping stopped. Crunching of toast—then silence. All eyes on Anne-Marie now. We held our breath. "Sure, OK," she said. Clapping resumes. . . "Sure, Ok, but . . ." Bretons climb down. *Total* silence this time.

"No, see, it was like this. (Her eyes flash a different colour!) Granda fought Franco in Spain, then got back in time for Hitler. I reckoned that Franco should meet face-to-face the grand-daughter of a poor man who spent some of the best years of his life fighting against a rich man who has just now died, pampered in his bed. Franco would have had to look me in the eye but he'd have been fed the toast and black pudding like everyone else so I phoned the Spanish embassy in London and told them about our party here. I said if the Generalissimo could make it we'd offer a sleeping bag and some floor space."

Anne-Marie, *my* cousin. Relief. She had wanted Francisco Franco here but *not* because she liked him. She wanted to face him down. Anne-Marie had always been determined. Like the time she turned up on our doorstep in Glasgow at 5 am, arriving alone from Dublin, for a *quick visit* she said. She was ten years old!

The students were saying, "fancy a swim in the canal?" It was cold November but the Bretons began to strip—the girl down to lime green pants and a bra, the boy down to a pair of boxer shorts covered with the Quebecois flag. Heaps of toast kept piling up in the hatch. Hot butter and crumbs of black pudding dribbled down chins. A couple of fiddlers were giving laldy to "The Jig of Slurs," "Scarce o Tatties" and "The Mason's Apron."

Anne-Marie walked into the centre of the room, tall in her green tweed skirt and cowboy shirt with white doves on a field of blue. She stood under a lone light bulb which set her hair off like a rainbowed oil slick. Silence for the last time.

"Franco is dead. *Requiescat in pace*. . . We are gathered here mainly to eat, drink and talk about hurling, horse racing and other, lesser religions. As you know, The Generalissimo couldn't make it and will now *never* make it but then neither could Granda."

Amen to Granda Gallagher said Walshie, his Roman helmet in hand, head bowed.

General sniggering. The girl in lime green knickers shivered from the cold. . .

Anne-Marie continued. "Granda died of lung cancer at the age of 82, the same age as Franco today, so there is some justice in the world."

The fiddle had stopped, the eating and slurping stopped too. Our thought was a collective one, a collective question voiced silently in English, Irish and Breton.

What about the cigarette lighter? What about the cigarette lighter?

And Anne-Marie, always clued in, caught the silver Tinkerbell of that thought as it hovered in the smoke-filled room.

"Ah, the cigarette lighter."

(Well, we all supposed it only killed Granda (with lung cancer) so it didn't really kill just fascists because granda was *anti-fascist*.)

Anne-Marie tilted her head forward, the curls spilling over her front like a black waterfall. She reached into her skirt pocket. She held silver lighter up to the light bulb.

"*The* cigarette lighter," she said.

She lit a candle on the table. Someone turned off the lights. The circle pressed forward, Spanners, Walshie, the shivering Bretons, Mickey Flamingo (with fiddle), myself, the woman from County Clare and others.

Lighter in one hand, hands folded in front.

"Let us pray. Granda who is in heaven—or at least *deserves* to be there rather than anywhere else. Thy name we humbly praise.

Francisco Franco is finally dead. Your cigarette lighter has worked in mysterious ways. Amen."

We all repeated *Amen.*

Then the Bretons danced on the table Mickcy fiddled. Joe Spanners then wondered aloud if Franco had died without *ever* tasting sweet crumbs of black pudding, toast and ketchup between his teeth.

Fly Fishing from Peterhead Prison

He arrived in New York with a shilling in his pocket—my Granda. He was an unemployed cabinet maker from Glasgow. He landed during the McCarthy era and was not certain how his socialist views would fare overseas; he was nearly fifty years old, arriving in the Land of Youth.

"First," he said, leaning back in his leather easy chair, "private property should be abolished."

I didn't understand this since he didn't have any private property in Scotland and had come to America to get some. He now had a house and a car as well as some wood-working tools which he could never afford in Scotland.

"Aye, not personal wealth but the huge wealth generated by oil companies and aristocrats."

He then launched into his predictable litany of villains: Winston Churchill, Wimpey Construction Company, the Greeks, Eamonn de Valera (that bluidy "Cuban") and others. Goodies were few: Keir Hardie, Grace the Cricketer, Harry Lauder and John MacLean. Granda had met both Keir Hardie and Sir Harry Lauder and was impressed with both of them. His own father had taken him to see Keir Hardie give a lecture on the evils of drink. A drunken heckler was silenced when Hardie told him that social change rarely happened face down in the mud, choking on your own vomit.

Later, I read about John MacLean and James Connolly. I knew my Granda's views were inconsistent. A boy, though, didn't really care about Marx or Harry Lauder. Granda's salmon fishing interested me more. "The right to a salmon is every man's right," he said firmly.

Granda is long since dead, buried in the middle of America in a graveyard bordered by rustling corn where redwing black-birds trill with that syrupy warble that words can't tell: the gurgle of life itself. Over the fence from the graveyard are plenty of honeybees seeking the honeysuckle there. He knew about bees too, and talked often about them. He hoped that men could learn the rules of society from the way bees lived and worked. But while he lived it was fishing not politics we had in common and we scouted for places for him to fly fish, not easy to do in mid-America where trout and salmon were scarce or many hours drive away.

Anyway, we'd found an abandoned gravel pit where bluegill and bass came to the surface flies, so Granda was happy. I could spin for big pike which made me happy. Two foreigners fishing away on a hot summer's night, light years from the coalfields of Lanark where Granda earned his first wage at the age of thirteen.

The old gravel pit machines were rusting and crumbling, but looked sleek and new in the twilight. We heard the crescendo of cicadas, the eternal fiddling of crickets and katydids. Goldfinches glided to the thistles, fireflies twinkled in the cornfields. The deep pit water was alive with bullfrog bellowing.

Then, a car pulled up, disturbing our peace. A fat man with a thin face jumped out and thrust his face close to my Granda's. Granda was quietly tying a fly and humming "The Flooers o' the Forest." The man shouted "Are you deaf or something?"

Granda never looked up as he spoke quietly to the man.

"You say this pit is yours but I've never needed permission to fish here before."

The veins stood out on the shouting man's neck. They looked like worms, wet under the sweat.

"We'll see about that. I'll phone the police. Why, that pit is deep and dangerous. If that boy fell in and drowned, I could be sued down to my last penny!"

Granda winked at me, and then looked at the man properly for the first time.

"If that boy fell in and drowned, he would frighten the fish away and we'd have bugger all for our tea. The lad's no daft."

The man jumped back into his car, muttering about damned foreigners taking over his country. The tyres threw up dust which sprinkled on the surface of the clear water.

Granda continued fishing, slow and sure. The fish rose to every fly as they must have done when he was a young man in Scotland. The moon painted glistening strokes across him and his fly rod. His mind was far, far away from me, the gravel pit, the angry man and even all the fish we had both caught.

Later, he told me during the long drive home that while the fat man was threatening him with the police, he was thinking only of John MacLean on hunger strike long ago in a Scottish jail so that men could be free the world over; even free to fish in deep water thousands of miles away from the iron bars of Peterhead Prison.

Gaps in My CV

Big Jessie is always clear about what she wants and when.

"I want my biscuit. I SAID I WANT MY BISCUIT... I WANT MY..."

I give her a biscuit. It's not allowed but I've been here long enough to know what to do. I'm a patient, same as Jessie but I like to think the resemblance ends there. I don't need a biscuit. I don't even like biscuits. See, I like to keep myself fit for the work I need to do. Yes. Work. Even here. Plenty to be getting on with. I've got to stay fit, keep my brain ticking over.

Harry the Orderly and me have an understanding. He gives us our medications, and we pass time the best we can. I have time to think about time. The Grandfather Paradox, Novikov's Self-Consistency Principle and other time stuff.

"How's it going Time Man?"

"Not so bad, Harry, not so bad. Life is short but work is long and we're a long time dead, Harry, so we are."

Harry takes one of my biscuits. Also not allowed but Harry can see the sense in bending a few rules. Wasting a bit of time after medication break.

"Simply put, Harry, if I travel back in time, I wouldn't be able to alter anything. For example, I could not tamper with my father's birth or his father's life which prevents my birth, therefore prevents my going back in time, having never reached the future in order to go back in the past."

"Hey, youse, put back those dominoes," shouts Harry to some patients across the room. "You were saying?"

"That's the classic Grandfather Paradox. You can't travel in time because it would interrupt what has already happened. And this allows for closed timelike curves, another important consideration when I finally finish my time studies."

"So why didn't you kill Hitler like you planned?"

"Ah, but Harry, I did try. It was 1938. Just like Kennedy in Dallas. I had a good safe spot picked out. An easy head shot. But a little kid was helped up to see the Fuhrer better and it ruined my chance. The cavalcade continued and I had to run." Harry looks bewildered. Another round of medication. Toilets. Big Jessie is roaring her head off for a chocolate biscuit so I re-group my thoughts while Harry is distracted. Most people would be interested in what I have to say so I sometimes can't fathom Harry's indifference.

"Do you have any biscuits left, son? For Big Jessie?" I hand him a pack.

Harry's ok. He pretends to follow my reasoning but he is a bit limited. This time stuff is way off his radar. I tried to kill Stalin too but slipped on some bloody ice, just as my shot zinged past. I barely escaped the Secret Police by slipping into a time worm-hole in a quiet corner of the Kremlin.

I also had a business plan for Third Lanark Football Club which would have kept them solvent and playing football for-ever, but I was late getting to their offices on account of an anti-Vietnam parade. So it goes. See you can't waste time without injuring eternity. A theory of mine.

Harry returns. He has a big splodge of ketchup down his shirt and coffee stains down his trousers. Bet it was Big Jessie. Throws stuff when things don't go her way. I tried my theories out on Big Jessie when I first came here. I thought she was inter-ested but I suppose it was just my biscuits she cared about.

"I've got to go now Jessie, to kill Hitler and prevent World War Two."

"Did they have biscuits in World War Two?"

"Fine biscuits, good biscuits Jessie. The best."

"Bring me some."

"Will do."

I did, except the biscuits themselves hadn't really travelled in time. I gave some of my allowance money my mum gives me to Harry. He fetched them at the 24 Hour Shopadrome round the corner. I told Jessie the biscuits were from another dimension.

Jessie's maw opened. The biscuits went down the shoot. You know, like kids down the flumes at the pool. Jessie wasn't inter-ested in Hitler or Stalin, just the biscuits and she wouldn't care if they came from Auschwitz or some Siberian gulag.

Anyway. I finally proved the Grandfather Paradox which states that I can't go back in time and alter anything. I didn't want to tamper with my grandfather's life so I did something simple. I went back in time to one family Christmas. I stole the Christmas turkey so that there would be no turkey, allowing them no time to get another one and cook it. Then, I shot back to Christmas but there the turkey was! Proving you can't mess with time. One *cannot* alter time. But I also once got stranded out in what the physicists call "an ensemble of parallel universes" one of which clearly had our family sitting around complaining that some bastard had nicked their Christmas turkey bawling *Where the hell was it and who would do such a thing?* But that event is in a parallel universe, in a completely separate timeline. So time can be altered but not in our *own* timeline. Somewhere, there could be a universe where I did assassinate Hitler or Stalin. Parallel time string, parallel universe, only one of several billion possibilities.

Today I have an idea. I will travel back in time and put various bets on the Grand National, the European Cup, and the World Cup. When I collect the money, I'll share it out a bit with some of my friends here, and then scarper for good.

Now I'm ready. Back to Munich, 1938. A rally. Hitler Youth. Today I will shoot the little bastard, dive into my closed timeline curve wormhole and return to read what history says about it. They introduced him to the audience. Just when he raised an arm I shot him just above the moustache; a clean shot and I tell you the little shit went down. Pandemonium. Storm troopers running everywhere. My time wormhole was just behind a cigarette kiosk. I heard shots ricocheting above my head. I dived in.

I got back just in time for medication and evening television. The newscaster was animated.

"Although it is widely assumed that Hitler died by his own hand in his private Berlin bunker, this very day new evidence has just come to light that Hitler may actually have been assassinated in Munich in 1938, and that an impostor was substituted for the Fuhrer from then for the duration of the war, in one of the Third Reich's most carefully guarded secrets. The assassin was never caught but was thought to be a local student who was part of a leftwing conspiracy. He was never identified or found."

Harry switches off the TV and starts to make some hot chocolate. Jessie is howling. "I WANT A FIG ROLL AND I WANT IT NOW!" Nobody even mentions the newscast.

It is hard to work in such an environment. I hope they will fully appreciate me one day.

A good day's work though. Tomorrow, I need to shore up my theory of Novikov's Self Consistency Principle, with some further research into closed time like curves and ensembles of parallel universes but now it's time to queue up for my medication. I need some quiet time now.

Tomorrow is another day but that is the future. I have no future and won't go there unless I have to. The past I understand. It is safer. We know exactly where we stand with the past.

The Show

It didn't look like a real person at first. It looked like clothes just blown off a washing line and landing, crumpled, in the field. From another angle it looked like a newborn lamb. There, just behind the last car.

Donnie sends the cars up the field, towards me. I direct them to park so that when the show is over, people can leave without boxing each other in. Big space, a row, and then another row, bumper to bumper. The first row drives forward, the row behind it reverses. Nobody trapped, nobody boxed in. *Parking stewards* we're called, with yellow safety jackets on so people can see us over the rise of the field so won't run over us. Sometimes the cars just park where they think best and usually they get it right.

Several cars are coming over the rise. The show will start soon and these are latecomers. I motion with my right arm *come on come on that's it* and then point to the parking space with my left hand. One car next to another, as close to the other cars as possible. When people leave the cars, they are smiling. They have found a parking place. There is nothing else to worry about now. Having parked, they can now enjoy the show. Men, women, children, dogs. All going to the show to enjoy themselves.

It is going well, the rain is holding off but there is a lull. I can hear birds singing that the noise of the cars had drowned out. And that's when I first see the bundle of clothes. But it is not a bundle. It is a woman. I can see that clearly now. She sits at the back of her car, in the grass, slumped, sitting in a yoga position, head down. She is sobbing quietly. Her whole body is shaking. Then she begins to cry more loudly.

There is a man next to her, hovering above her. He has his left arm out, as if to touch her hair, but he does this like a man approaching to catch a wasp on a window. He hesitates. Moves slightly. No, maybe not like approaching a wasp but more like a man trying to catch a butterfly, without hurting it, without breaking its wings.

He stays just like that. I move closer. He has this look, like, like *What do I do? Please, what do I do? What is the right thing to do?* The woman is still sobbing. She has on a pinkish t-shirt and jeans. Her hair is sort of straw-coloured, reddish. She is slender, small, childlike. He is tall, in chinos, his shoes too clean for a muddy field.

I want her to speak. To say something like *you bastard, go away, get away from me* or *I'm sorry I'm just upset* but it is worse because she is not speaking. She is in her own world, and the man is in the same world I'm in, we're both in. But she is in another place, and could be there for a long time. I should do something. I am young; the man is as old as my father. The woman is maybe a bit younger than him, but older than me. I could say. *"Mam, can I help in any way? I could call for a stretcher. I have my mobile right here."* Or I could speak to her man. *"Sir, can I help? Do you need a doctor? A policeman? I know a bit of first aid,"* but Christ, it is not like that. It is worse than that. I can't say anything. It wouldn't seem right. It wouldn't help.

The man looks around, worried, worried for himself because his eyes show me that the woman is now beyond him, way beyond him. Her body is shaking and sobbing. She covers her eyes with her small hands, a gold ring on her finger.

She has shrunken into a small ball, a tiny bundle of clothes.

The men who walk past put their arms around their women or children, sensing unease. They walk faster past the man, whose arm is still suspended. The women hesitate when they see the crumpled woman, but the men seem to nudge the women along, to move away. To move away quickly.

The woman is now so small against the cars, the field and the sky full of oily tumbling storm clouds. A storm is coming. It was forecast and now, it is coming.

Then many cars come, in droves, to beat the storm. The woman is safe where she is sitting so I back-peddle, waving cars with my right arm, pointing to parking spaces with my left hand, *park here, that's it, park here, that's it, next to him.*

I forget the woman. She is way back in the field now. I check my watch. I can return my safety jacket. I am finished.

I walk into the show grounds. There is a lot going on. Old motorcycles, Nortons, Triumphs, BSAs. Engines and trucks and cars. Food stalls. I buy a burger with fried onions and a poke of chips with mayonnaise. But I can't eat. Can't focus. I want to see the woman and man, arm in arm, she laughing now, wiping away her tears, enjoying the stalls, the food, the vintage cars.

But I know I won't see them. It is getting dark. The show is over. I am walking home, afraid to look at the field. The cars have all filed out. I am afraid the man and woman may still be there, the woman sobbing and crying and the man with his arm cradled over her, still afraid to touch or speak, his hand hovering over her hair, like a small bird afraid to land.

Him not knowing what to do, still worried, not knowing what to do. Who to ask for help, knowing there can be no help. While she is slumped in that field, that lonely big field, in the dark, with storm clouds rolling in.

Demolition

Rain shook the hard reeds, ripping the bracken to bits. Mud poured from the hills, rolling stones into swollen burns. Two men were knocking down an old croft from the inside. The walls were stained green and brown from damp and mould. They worked at the cladding.

Jimmy moved the crowbar in short bursts. Bits of plaster, wood and rock crumbled onto his scuffed boots, which crunched shards of plaster under foot. The dust made a thin grey veil on the floor. The rain came in through missing slates and broken windows.

Kenny prised up the floorboards, most of them splitting where the woodworm had riddled them into tiny feathered patterns like the tips of bird wings. Each effort brought more of the fusty smell of earth into the dust and debris. Both men worked smoothly and quickly; each pry of the crowbar hastened the end of the ruin.

Then, Jimmy made a clean slice with the crowbar and two objects leapt from the wall and landed in the slush and rubble at his feet. Jimmy looked at Kenny who looked back. "Jesus Christ," they said in unison and both leaned back, laying their tools down. "Jesus Christ," they repeated and both sucked in a breath and began to roll a cigarette each. At their feet were two glistening objects, taller than either of the men. A black war shield and a ceremonial war mask bristling with large garish feathers of some exotic bird. Jimmy and Kenny stood back, fingering their cigarettes. "Mother of God," said Kenny, stubbing the cigarette out on the plaster-covered floor. The rain pelted down while four faces, two living and two freshly resurrected—wondered at this thing happening in another century far from the dusty African veldt where great lions still sleep in the sun, untroubled by cold Lochaber rain.

Gardens Strange and Cold

He has only just stepped from the bus and his wife is shouting at him. In front of everyone. More than an hour on a crowded bus, just home, and in front of everyone she is shouting at him. She is not angry though.

"Come quickly," she says, grabbing his hand like a child would do. "Hurry."

"Have you every seen anything like this?" she asked, pointing to the gable wall of their house. He looked. He hadn't.

The gable end of the council house is white harl, set against the blue June sky. The yellow broom is ablaze on the green hill, looking like blisters on the sloping back of the land. He bends down to look more closely at what he thinks he has seen. To make sure.

The creature is bigger than his big workingman's hand.

"A butterfly?" she says.

"No, I think it's a moth."

It is shivering and distressed, beating its wings against the wall.

She looks at the moth, then at him.

"We can't leave it here. The neighbourhood cats will kill it. We'll bring it inside, poor wee soul."

He thinks. She is like that. Everything in the world is her poor wee soul. He has always liked that kindness about her.

"Fetch my cigar box. It's nearly empty anyway."

The cigar box has a picture of Prince Edward on it. With his big hands he guides, nearly scoops, the moth into the box and closes the lid. They put the box near the gas fire while they have their tea.

"Yon creature is a wonder," she speaks over the soft sound of chewing and working forks.

"Not a wonder from here. Not by a long way. There is no creature like that in these islands."

"Will it live?"

He's not sure. "I don't think they have mouth parts for feeding. It's the caterpillars that feed. Adults mate and die."

After a cup of tea, he lifted the lid of the box. The creature was dead. They marvel at the size of it and the colour of the wings. In their combined century of Scottish life, they have never seen so many colours as are on the wing of the moth.

He takes the bus to work in Edinburgh only three days a week now, working in a dying trade. He makes miniature furniture for exhibitions and displays. He carves the wood and paints the intricate detail. More and more of the work is mass-produced and made in man-made materials. He admits some of it looks better than his work. It costs less too. On the bus he puts his leather tool bag on the net rack above the seat and carries the cigar box on his knee.

The museum is not far from his work and he has an hour for lunch.

The young man at the museum is sniffy at first.

"A moth. Yes, we have many moths already." He opens the box impatiently, expecting something that it isn't there. He changes his tone, like an engine moving up a gear.

"Where did you find this?"

"Yesterday. Teatime. It was clinging to the gable end of my council house. It was still alive."

The young man cleared his throat.

"May I keep this until Dr Wilson comes back this afternoon?"

"You may keep it forever if you like. Display it so others can see it. It is a wonder, right enough."

He went back and finished his afternoon's work, a copy of a Duncan Phyfe chair.

He took the bus home having been told his firm would fold in a month's time. Something he had been expecting when his work week was cut from five days to three. He would be given handsome severance pay

The bus moved through the June countryside, sun, green hills, cobalt sky, cold enough to let all the colours blend in a vibrant way. The grass shivered on the hill, the way the moth shivered.

He went back to the museum the following week.

The same young man greeted him.

"Dr. Wilson said your moth was a long way from home. It comes from the Atlas Mountains of Morocco. It may have been a stowaway with fruit or vegetables but chances are the southern winds blew it here. With your permission, we will display it in our cases adding your name to the information."

"No keep the moth but leave my name out. My name is not important."

He has a relative in New York who will sponsor him. He will go out alone, leaving his wife with her son in Edinburgh. He, being an old merchant navy man, will sail to New York.

He went through immigration with his tool bag and it being morning, decided he would walk to his nephew's apartment. He would ask directions.

The moth was in his head, even in New York. He thought of its shivering, its colours. He remembered a line from an old poem. "To sleep in Gardens, strange and cold." Both man and moth.

The Golden Book of Scottish Vanishings - Continued

Scottish aunties Margaret and Jean (are there any other kind?) at required times produced Jeddart Snails, Hawick Balls and other sweets and boilings. They have vanished but they gave me an idea I am still working on. Auntie Jean wanted to write this book about Scots who had done vanishing acts but it never got beyond her notes in a shorthand book. She was good at Gregg's shorthand so I had to have it "translated."

BRIGADOOM
Brigadoom was a horrible place. Full of neds and alcoholics, violence and self-righteousness. Prods hated Catholics. People had a terrible diet and both men and women walked around displaying tattoos under rolls of flesh the colour of beef dripping. It was such a terrible place that a curse had been put on it to remove it into a parallel universe. When two Americans stumbled on the place, they were reduced to slobbering idiocy for wanting to escape. They had only been there for ten minutes. Brigadoom is quite a big place – exactly the same size and population as Scotland. It only comes to life for one day every hundred years which is probably best for the world as a whole. Lots of music has been written about it to deal with its pet themes of violence, bigotry, alcoholism and very bad teeth.

HARE, WILLIAM
In Portobello my mum sang
  "Up thi close, doon thi stair
  In thi hoose with Burke and Hare
  Burke's the butcher, Hare's thi thief . . ."
Hare was pretty proud that he never robbed graves. Murder yes, but he stooped at grave robbing. He and his wife Margaret helped Burke and his mistress Helen murder 16 or 17 people depending on who you believe. Since the only witnesses had been killed, Hare bought his life by testifying against William Burke and Helen. Burke was hung in January 1828 and Hare was released in February. He vanished although many rumours circulated about a death in Ireland, the North of England or London, sometime around 1860. His wife Margaret and Helen both went their separate ways but were hounded and stoned

wherever they went; Margaret to Ireland and Helen Burke to Australia. Hare went God knows where. Maybe he and his pal Willie Burke ended up, ultimately, in the same place?

JOCK O HAZELDEAN
The bride diznae like the man her faither is forcing her to marry. She fancies Jock O Hazeldean instead. All these rich fowk are lined up for the wedding in a muckle hall. The feast is ready. The bride has other ideas, a bit like in The Graduate but instead of the bus, she is up on Jock's horse, into folklore. It rocks. Aye.

JOHN JEFFREY (1826-1854)
The young man from Perth worked hard in the Edinburgh Botanical Gardens so they sent him to Canada and America to gather plants and seeds for the Botanic Garden. In 1850 and 1851 he sent back many crates. He last shipped plant seeds in 1854 then was never heard from again. He disappeared. Murdered. Died of thirst or hunger, ran off to the gold rush. His seeds and plants lived after him. Think of him next time you see a Jeffrey Pine.

JAMES LITTERICK (1901-1942?)
A Communist from Glasgow goes to Canada and stays a Communist. In 1940 the Communist Party is declared an illegal organisation and Litterick goes into hiding from the Royal Canadian Mounted Police. He is in a Montreal photo from 1942 but then was never heard from or seen again. Double agent? Safe house, new identity?

DONALD "GLOOMY MEMORIES" MACLEOD (1814-1857)
It would "make the very stones weep," said MacLeod about what happened to his people in Sutherland. They were cleared off and burned out, to make way for progress. People out, sheep in.

Harriet Beecher Stowe visited her friend the Duchess of Sutherland and called her book "Sunny Memories . . ." seeing no hypocrisy or irony in visiting a Duchess whose final solution wasn't much better than the slavery in America that Stowe detested. MacLeod, a Gaelic-speaking stonemason, taught himself to write in order to write in English a series of letters for the Edinburgh Weekly Chronicle about the Clearances in Sutherland. His writings appeared in a book in Toronto in 1857.

After that, MacLeod just faded away. It is rumoured that his own grave lies beneath a huge parking lot in Toronto.

PONTIUS PILATE

Once, a Scotsman saw Christ walking on water. He said: "See him, he cannae even swim!" The most famous Scot in history was probably Pilate who in legend was born under a Yew tree in Perthshire, in a Roman tent. Pilate said of Christ: "I find no fault in him." We know what happened to Christ but what became of Pilate?

He was thrown into the Tiber.

Thrown into the Rhone.

Committed suicide under orders from Tiberius.

Becomes Christian, lives in an Italian country cottage with his good wife Procla.

Another Scotsman who disappeared.

MICHAEL SCOT (T) 1175?-1234

Dante was scared shitless of this Borders man, who appeared and disappeared with regularity. Durham, Oxford, Paris. The common people feared him for his knowledge of the Black Arts.

خ د ذ ر ز س

ظ ط ض ص ش

ك ق ف غ ع

They saw these strange symbols in his book, though it was probably only his Arabic writing. Scot conjured up fancy food from thousands of miles away, with the touch of a magic wand. He split the Eildon Hills into three with one strike of the same wand, even though the Romans called the same hills Trimontium a thousand years before. Here, there, vanishing. Dante stuck him in the Eighth Circle of Hell from where Michael Scot would easily escape. A bit like Elvis really. Scot now works in a chip shop in Coldstream.

JOHN JAMES WATERSTON (1811-1883?)

Waterston was a physicist and engineer. He worked in India for nearly twenty years and helped set up the great Indian railway system. He was also a physicist who was way ahead of his time.

On 18th June 1883, he went out for his normal stroll around Edinburgh and was never seen again! Some think he was washed into the sea near Leith by a huge wave. Others think he merely became giddy and fell in. He was such an intelligent man aliens may have needed his brain or his knowledge . . .

Meanwhile, the 'Disappearance' files on my desk are bulging. I'll never get through all of them. Unlike the people in the files, the files themselves show no danger of disappearing: aunties smelling of lavender, uncles buried deep under the mud of the Somme, rich men and commoners, wizards, seed collectors, you, me, rough sleepers in London and small children last seen alive at the fun fair.

Teething Pains

I remember the Holy Water, the monkey and the jet beads. The Holy Water is gone and the monkey is dead but I have the beads.

Two blocks and seventy years separated us — down a cavern of tenements, up a short flight of steps from the pavement, then into a door peeling in great green blisters. I was sent to take messages to my great aunt: baking soda for cleaning Devlin's false teeth (her husband was always just *Devlin* — I never knew his Christian name), sugar for Devlin's tea, but best of all — spices for Devlin's curry, for there wasn't much curry being eaten in those days.

The door opened to a long dark hall, with several more doors, all green, all peeling like dead skin. There was a coat rack on the right and at the same height, an ornamental font of Holy Water. Next to the font was a plaster Holy Virgin. She was lime green. Hung on the coat rack was a green and white Hibs scarf which said CHAMPIONS 1902-1903.

Bella snorted: "Devlin's scarf *nae* mine. Dinnae cross yerself. Ye're nae ane o *them*." (A young girl, I didn't yet know who *them* were.)

Bella, as big across as tall, face ruddy, huge forearms the colour of corned beef but the one thing you always noticed: her eyes, like deep dark sloes; eyes which somehow didn't belong with the rest of her face, as they glistened like dark beads. But I never got beyond that door or into the sitting room, where I imagined Devlin sitting in an unravelling cardigan, in soiled baffies with the toes missing.

I was too young to know why she married *ane o them* but my own aunt told me later.

"Like Bella, Devlin was born out in India, in the jute trade. He came back to Leith but planned to go back to the trade and Bella married him because she was desperate to go back *tae the Ghats*, as she called it. Devlin got steady work at the warehouse so he never went back. They couldn't have children for some medical reason."

Bella showed me a certificate once, with huge red seals on it like flattened roses. Her mother grew up in Bengal and was married at 14 to a lad from Her Majesty's 44th, who himself wasn't much older than that. It was all on the certificate, including her own name, *Isabella Reidpath*.

Bella's father died at 16 from a sniper's bullet, and the young widow boarded a ship with her child. Bella's mother had more than gone native, speaking Bengali to her daughter and the girl's first words in Leith were not Scots ones either. Bella pulled her hair back native fashion and walked down Lorne Street barefoot; when teased or upset, she always cried aloud in Bengali.

Devlin's family lived just up the street but with the jute industry in a slump and with the betting shops and his beloved Hibernian Football Club just around the corner, Devlin gradually forgot about India. Meanwhile, Bella's adult life became more of a sullen nightmare as her Indian dream retreated further down the grey streets until it melted back into the tenements, in the cold autumn rain.

"Oh, aye, Bella likes her curry so she does. Just you run along with this wee poke."

Wee poke in the cold rain. I can still smell it: cardamom, cinnamon, coriander, cumin, turmeric. I skipped to those names:

Curry powder, curry powder,
Cardamom, cardamom,
Yer mammies greetin, aye greetin,
intae a poke o cinnamon.

Despite Bella's bitterness at Devlin, her curry was the one thing they still shared. I remember thinking; there is a song behind those black eyes:

Farewell Ichalkaranji, Dharwad, The Ghats,
dark Brahmaputra and the turquoise sea,
the sugar sand of Goa, Ethiopia, Egypt,
whispering Sudan and Araby.

Great whales diving, porpoises singing,
up from Suez, up from Suez,
oh dark birds winging.

Devlin died, and my visits were few (for it had only been Devlin who needed sugar for his tea) but there were always the spices, and "odd wee bits for the monkey."

The *monkey*. Where did it come from? Did she always have it, even pre-Devlin? Some say Devlin kept it exiled "ben the hoose," others say she bought it to replace "that other ape" — Devlin himself.

One frosty day I went to the door and saw the beast above the coat rack. Devlin's font was gone now but the monkey was chewing a filthy and tattered Hibs scarf. The monkey had big bright coppery eyes, bigger than an old penny. It stood only a foot high and was tailless. It was brown above and silver grey underneath. The creature's nose was huge, as were its rounded ears. Its long fingers were wrapped around the coat rack. A few words in an Indian tongue and it retreated, dragging Devlin's old scarf into the sitting room. The monkey smelled of something like piss or the spray of an old tomcat.

I didn't really like that monkey so it was a good thing Bella never asked me in and never offered me a biscuit or tea or juice so I was always able to hurry away. Up to the Macdonald Road library to look up *monkey* in the books. I found it. A "Slender Loris," native of Southern India or Tibet, belonged to the swamps and forests there. *Loris Tardigradus*, nocturnal, slow-moving, feeding on insects and small lizards. Nicknamed the "urine-washing" monkey because it helped define its territory by trailing its urine scent everywhere it went. (Not exactly Devlin's *holy water*.)

My aunt told me *I* was the lucky one, if the monkey was called off when I went there. It seems Bella taught the beast to piss on command. One Bengali word and the monkey would piss on the socks, shoes, or stockings of the offending visitor: any friend of Devlin's, Hibs supporters, salesmen, ministers and any *o them*. Bella had few visitors.

The *beads*. When Devlin was alive, Bella always wore them. They matched her eyes exactly and I always thought they were some kind of prayer beads. She worried them, rubbed them. I know about them now:

Albert Prince of Saxe-Coburg-Gotha died in 1861, and as the Empire went daft with mourning, jet beads became all the rage. This shiny lignite fossil—found in graves in Palaeolithic times and much loved in the Bronze Age as a talisman—polished beautifully, what's more, the beads were English to the core since the best jet deposits were from the Upper Lias of Whitby; a big industry as long as the stubborn Queen mourned for her man but in time, the craze ended and the jet veins closed (Spain took over the jet trade) but at the height of an Empire in mourning, the young child Bella began cutting teeth somewhere off black Africa on board ship and her teenage mother offered the sloe-eyed child black beads to chew on, to ease the pain from one world to another one, and the girl left tiny teeth marks, like a fossil imprint; those rough ridges would be fingered by that same hand nearly ninety years later.

But when Devlin died, the monkey was given the beads, and one of my last visits to the door found me crawling around the dark hall, looking for beads scattered when the monkey had chewed through the rawhide string holding them together. I found them all, under the gaze of the beast who now only had one filthy corner of Devlin's Hibs Scarf left, the bit that said *1902*.

I wasn't there at the very end. I was told it was a February day, pelting with a cold rain, when my aunt went over with some curry spices. She chapped on the door. No reply. She went back over in the evening with her man. The house was dark, although a fire should have been on in the grate, visible from the street. They finally forced the door.

They called out. No reply. They went into the sitting room. No fire. No-one there. They walked down the hall. Opened each door. Scullery dark, teacup still full of tea. Then to the last door, the bedroom. The room was dark. They lit the gaslight.

The old woman was propped up in bed. Her bed was covered with statues of elephant gods and of blue deities with many arms. Bella's dark eyes were closed. Her long hair had been brushed out but plaited, Indian fashion.

She wore a native silk dressing gown, which hung limp on her wasted frame. And among all the gods and dervishes on her bed, in the centre, was the monkey stuffed and mounted like a museum piece, a tiny rag of green and white clutched in its fingers.

And on Bella's neck were the jet beads, her toothless mouth clamped firmly around them.

The Bridge Keeper's Log Book.
Incident number 9361.

My work booth is the size of a small caravan. There is a smaller separate room with flush toilet and basin. I have a phone and desk. I phone in some repairs.

"I think the rivets are going in section three. Better have a look."

The guys come and have a look.

"Right, mate, we'll replace the whole panel. Well-spotted."

I have a long window facing the bridge. Cars and motor-cycles only. No big lorries, bicycles or pedestrians. Nearly everything is grey but my office is white. I have a cork bulletin board and a calendar from a local restaurant, featuring English landmarks. This month's photo is of the Angel of the North. Emergency phone numbers are pinned on the board.

"Hello. This is the bridge man. Some rubbish has fallen onto the northbound lane. Better clear it. Could be dangerous."

"I'll send a guy right away."

"Thanks."

That kind of thing.

My hours are ten at night to six in the morning, graveyard shift. There is a small fridge and an electric kettle. Teabags. Instant coffee. Milk. Sugar. It's all there. All a man on this job needs.

First thing, boil the kettle. Two spoonfuls of instant coffee. I then add the milk and two sugars. A digestive biscuit. About 2 a.m. I make a sandwich and have another coffee.

Nothing happens, but.

It's 3 a.m. a guy is knocking at the door. I bang on the window. He comes to the window. Not much traffic. A well dressed guy, suit, long coat. Carries a briefcase.

"This is not a pedestrian bridge," I shout.

"I'm not a pedestrian."

"Look like one to me, sunshine. What's the trouble? Can I call a garage?"

"Let me in."

"It's against the rules."

"Then fuck your rules."

He whispers this. He sets the briefcase on the outside window ledge, and then walks out of the range of my vision.

I think about this for a few minutes, then phone the police.

"There's a guy acting strange out on the bridge. He's on foot."

They arrive quickly. I'm allowed to let the police in. They empty his briefcase out on my desk. Some photos land among some coffee stains. The coffee mugs stains remind me of that Olympic logo, all looped together.

The photos are of the man and a pretty woman with dark hair and eyes. There are also two children in the photo, a little boy and girl, also with dark hair and eyes though they have the man's look, a kind of wanting *to hide* look. That's all that's in the briefcase. They leave it on my desk then walk out along the bridge, with their torches shining. Not much traffic now. It's after 4 a.m. so I make a coffee and sandwich. Cold meat tonight.

Police come back.

"Didn't see anything but we'll phone a boat. We'll take the briefcase too. Give us a ring if you see or hear anything else."

They leave. I finish the coffee. Eat the cold meat. Look at the calendar. I am sick of the Angel of the North and steal a look at the next month's picture. It's just another bridge, down south somewhere.

Like I say, it's a good job. Pays well. Nothing much happens. Nothing that really matters anyway.